Where Did This Come From?

Third Edition

by

Larry Nocella

Where Did This Come From? Third Edition is a work of fiction.

Where Did This Come From? Third Edition
Copyright 2013 by Larry Nocella

ISBN-13: 978-0615817163
ISBN-10: 0615817165

Published by QECE Publishing
www.LarryNocella.com

This ebook file prepared May 2013

Cover design by Tom Demi

*The author would like to thank Tom Demi for proofreading.
Any remaining errors are my own. – LN*

Other works by Larry Nocella

Loser's Memorial (a novel)

It Never Goes Away (short story)

Where Did This Come From?

Third Edition

by

Larry Nocella

BOOK I

Part 1

1

Brrraaaaaapppppp!

A belch ripped through the silent Palaguan river valley and bounced off the lush green walls of the canyon. Laughter followed it. The belcher bowed to his admirers and guzzled another martini, half of which he spilled on his Hawaiian shirt.

Seen from above, the river was a still black line, tracing a wandering course through deep green spotted with clouds. Its path described no pattern, as if it were made by a great god doodling, dragging her finger idly through the dark jungle. On this black line, moving slowly, was the tiny white speck of a tour boat where the belcher took his bows.

"The remaining rainforest is in pristine condition. Nearly as it was since pre-historic times," the boat's tour guide said into her microphone, her voice crackling through the barely functioning speaker system.

Brrraaaaaapppppp!

Belches announced their coming. Belches from the engine, belches from the passengers. The tour boat floated down the river, jungle creatures scurrying into the green blackness before it, running from the sound and smell.

A handful of passengers sat on a bench at the front of the boat, straining to hear the tour narrative, crowded near Nina Vasquez and her microphone. The bulk of tourists were massed in the rear at the bar, enjoying the belching contest.

"Some of these trees are over--" Nina's voice was cut short by thunderous cackling and whooping. She kept talking, rolling her eyes, her contempt hidden behind sunglasses.

"--years old. They are capable of--"

Another monstrous belch ripped the air. Two of those on the front bench looked over their shoulders, glaring toward the drunken crowd.

The boat rumbled on. Nina kept talking, disconnecting herself, allowing her consciousness to float away while she conducted the tour. Those few nearby, that minority of tourists intent on listening to the naturalist on this nature cruise, leaned forward. The static-impaired loudspeaker wasn't enough to cut through the party in the back.

Nina was jaded. This situation no longer enraged her, and she ceased to wonder with frustration why the tourists always wore Hawaiian shirts, despite the fact they were in South America.

A woman from the front row bolted up, stiffened her back and stomped to the rear of the boat. "Can you please keep it down back here?" she said, her head shaking. "We're trying to listen to the tour."

The partiers nearest her fell silent, but deeper into the throng, she couldn't be heard, or was being ignored.

She turned around and stomped back up the aisle. A balled-up cocktail napkin bounced off the back of her head.

"Oooh," the partiers growled in a low whoop, the standard "someone is in trouble" observation of crowds. Shrill laughter followed and the party was back in swing seconds later. The woman sat down on the bench, folded her hands, closed her eyes and took a deep breath. She looked up at Nina as if nothing had happened.

"Can't you do something about them?" a man asked.

Nina stared at him for an instant, shrugged, and continued talking.

* * *

It was another day at work, preaching to the few who wanted to listen but who couldn't hear. Nina had ceased to feel sorry for them and she knew better than to stop serving drinks. The booze was what kept her in business.

"Can't you please say something?" someone on the front bench asked. "You do have the microphone. We paid you good money."

Safe behind her sunglasses, Nina said nothing, pretending she hadn't heard. She had learned long ago that it was futile, even made the situation worse, trying to silence people who thought they deserved whatever they wanted and were drunk.

Flicking used-up cigars into the water, the older men at the back flirted with a young, tight-skirted girl. They bought her drinks and caressed her hair. Their wives gathered in a corner, muttering "slut" into their cocktails. Nina observed that the same young girls showed up often, conspicuous among the elderly tourists. Back in the days Nina had cared, she was upset that she was assisting the local Palaguan prostitutes. Now, she felt a cynical satisfaction that at least someone was getting something out of the tour.

She rationalized well. Some things were so inevitable, so irresistible, they may as well be natural events like storms or earthquakes. Complaining didn't help. Fighting was impossible. It was best to focus her energies on how to endure.

She dealt by ignoring.

That's why her eyes stayed focused on the deep forest. Only its dark thick green, almost black with mystery, gave her solace. Despite the embarrassing noise of the party and the boat, the natural insulation dampened the sound. She was certain she wouldn't have lasted if the river canyon echoed instead.

She imagined herself deep in that green-blackness, safe, silent, far away.

The boat rumbled down the calm river as she continued to speak from memory.

"--territory of the Huapi tribe--"

Whooping cut her off. The young girl at the back was dancing with two white-haired men on either side. Both men, arms out, a drink in each hand, knees cautiously bent, fenced her in.

"Oooh baby!"

"--decimated by Spanish conquerors--"

"Get closer!"

"--generally shy. Rarely catch a gl--"

"Come to papa!"

"--culture dating back to 4,000 BC--"

Latin dance music scratched through the speakers.

"--now reduced to a population of slightly more than 100--"

Brrraaaaaapppppp!

2

The chief of the Huapi tribe snapped a piece of bark from a young tree and began chewing. He stared in the direction of the noisy, stinking boat and wondered to himself, "Where did this come from?"

The Huapi were a small tribe of nearly one hundred native South Americans whose numbers dwindled every year. The pace of newborns did not keep up with deaths. The tribe was further drained by those who stole away in the night to assimilate into mainstream Palaguan culture via the nearby Christian mission.

When the Huapi heard (and smelled) the tour boats coughing down the river near their small parcel of land, they would retreat into the jungle and wait for the noise to pass. All daily business and conversation stopped. Children cried as the white exhaust slid through the trees, burning their eyes and throats. The men looked around nervously, chewing bark, welcoming the relaxation brought on by its juices that kept their angry pride in check. Women waved leaves to drive the smoke away.

"This is our home," the chief, Maubombo, grumbled.

"Yes," his wife Yuala mumbled, barely paying attention. She was used to his testy outbursts when the boats came by. The rest of the tribe had done well learning to ignore or at least silently tolerate the noxious intrusion. She continued to weave a fruit-gathering basket without looking up.

"Then why should we hide?"

He rose.

His son, Ndiko, grabbed his arm. Smirking, he said, "Perhaps we should kill them, father. Perhaps today is different than the hundreds of other days the boat came by. Maybe today is the day you act instead of talk."

His mother frowned. "Don't push him."

The chief snapped his arm loose from his son. "Yes. Today is different." He strode into the center of the tiny circle of huts that made up the Huapi village.

"Now look what you've done." Yuala glared at her son. "Stop him. Please?"

Ndiko scowled and trudged after his father.

"Come on, all of you," the chief yelled, waving his arm over his head, signaling the men to follow. It was the same gesture he used when he led the hunt for the small mammals that made up part of the Huapi diet. Maubombo pushed the bark deeper into his mouth and lifted his spear. His chewing intensified. Reluctantly, the men stopped their daily tasks, grabbed their spears and followed after him.

Yuala glared at her snickering son as he disappeared into the jungle with his father.

3

Nina was speaking from rote, droning on about the mind-blowing facts and awesome living beauty of the jungle around them. She was looking to the side, staring into the jungle's dark when suddenly, the boat dipped to the right. She grabbed a railing reflexively, dropping her microphone.

"Paulo?" she called to the ship's captain in the cabin behind her. "What's happening?"

"I don't know. You tell me!" Paulo shouted over his shoulder, speaking Spanish. He leaned hard into the steering wheel to counter the weight-shift. The motor whined as it lifted out of the water.

The tourists were all moving to the right side of the boat, pointing.

"Please, everyone," Nina said, scooping up her microphone. "We need to balance the boat."

She looked to where the tourists were pointing.

A troop of Huapi was marching into a clearing. A dozen natives, naked except for their loincloths and painted bodies, were emerging from the jungle. Judging from his face markings, the leader of the column appeared to be the chief. He was striding down the incline to the tiny sandy beach, waving his fist and jabbing his spear.

Nina had been conducting tours in Palagua for three years, was a student of the land and its native peoples for far longer, but she had never seen such a fascinating procession. Her awe quickly gave way to vertigo as the boat lurched again.

"Paulo?"

"Tell them to spread out!" he shouted back.

Nina yelled into her microphone. "Please! Everyone! We need to balance the boat. Some of you please move to the other side!"

No one listened.

The dance music from the bar kept playing. Cameras flashed all along the boat's side, like a battleship shelling a coast.

"Please!" Nina said. "The Huapi do not like to have their pictures taken. They believe cameras steal their souls."

She hated telling a lie but she was becoming more desperate. No one was paying any attention to her, and the boat was tilting more sharply.

The flashes continued, so she tried a more direct approach.

"No pictures!" she screamed, her voice crackling over the speakers. She tapped a couple of her faithful tour-listeners and said, "Come with me."

She charged down the center aisle.

Years of frustration pushed through her apathy as she grabbed the nearest man in a Hawaiian shirt, ripped the camera from around his neck and threw it into the river.

"You bitch," he yelled. "That camera cost me three hundred bucks! I'm gonna sue!"

The old man shoved her. Nina's deputies meekly called out, "No pictures!" but they were of little help. Now it was their turn to abandon her. She waded into the field of Hawaiian shirts, grabbing at cameras, with little luck. Her blows were deflected. Someone even swung a punch at her. A martini splashed across her face.

"Move to the other side of the boat, now," she yelled.

The boat lurched again. A loud splash cut through the music.

"Man overboard!" someone shouted. The passengers started screaming.

Nina grabbed the railing, looking into the water where a bald head emerged. The partiers laughed and cackled all around her. Someone hurled a life-ring to him.

Cameras were still going off all along the side of the boat.

"There stand-um war chief," one photographer said to another. They both laughed, pointing.

"A photo this rare is probably worth something. It's not just stupid trees."

The chief was shaking his fist at them. The tourists shook their fists back. The Huapi men were now stretched in a line along the beach, taunting the tourists.

Nina threw up her arms. "You must move to the other side of the boat! We need to balance the boat or we'll all drown." A few of the tourists seemed to acknowledge her, but they stood on the benches, still firing away with their cameras, lancing the dark forest with strobe light.

"Stop taking pictures!" Nina yelled. She grabbed another camera and sent it to a wet grave.

"Hey!"

Nina ran back to the cabin. Speaking Spanish to Paulo, she said, "Can you get us out of here?"

"I'm trying but the motor's in the air!"

Nina stopped for a moment, mesmerized by what was happening in the clearing.

"Look at that," she said. "All these years and I've never seen so many Huapi all together."

She pulled her own camera from the steering room's drawer and aimed at the chief.

"What the hell are you doing?" Paulo yelled. "I need your help back there!"

"I only want one," she said, focusing the lens. She looked at the digital camera's preview screen.

"Nina! Come on!" Paulo yelled.

She sighted her camera on the chief and the Huapi surrounding him.

"Bull's-eye," she said, snapping the picture then hurling the camera back into the drawer.

"Okay, Paulo. What do you want me to do?"

"You done now? All finished?" Paulo asked. "Just get that guy back on board. Let's do that first."

"Someone threw a life ring. If we can get the boat moving, just drag him behind us. I want to get out of here."

"What about that other guy?" Paulo pointed to the shore but quickly returned his hand to the boat's wheel.

"What other guy?" Nina said, turning. What she saw made her jaw drop open.

The Huapi men had formed alongside their chief, watching the people on the boat shove and yell as the vessel thrashed in the water. Brilliant flashes of light burst from small devices the passenger carried. Half-heartedly at first, but his contempt growing, Chief Maubombo stood on the shore, pointing at the spectacle and cursing. The other Huapi followed his example.

"Look at them," the chief said. "The pales are fools! They can't-"

The bark he was chewing dropped into his throat, cutting off his breathing completely. He staggered back from the shore, falling behind his tribesmen who were distracted, jabbing their spears and gesturing at the boat partly out of hostility, partly out of bemused scorn. The flashing lights were frightening at first, but when they failed to harm anyone, they became a severe annoyance.

Behind his men, the chief clutched and punched at his throat, trying to dislodge the bark. He clawed at his neck, his pulse pounding through it into his palms. His mouth opened and closed, gasping for air, but gathering none. His eyes bulged until he thought they would burst.

Memories of the many fish he had caught flashed through his mind. So this is the pure panic they felt, unable to breathe, moments before their death.

The chief watched from behind as his tribe did his bidding by taunting the pales. He fell to his knees, dropped his spear, and began crawling toward their backs. He tried to call for help, but no sound emerged from his mouth. Spots exploded before his eyes and darkness crowded from the outside. Clumsy white people fell over the edge of the boat and splashed heavily into the river. He beat at his own chest, trying in vain to knock loose the bark.

5

"What the hell am I doing?" Joe Vera wondered as he waded onto the shore.

From his vantage point on the boat, as it had tipped upward, he could see above the Huapi crowd to the chief further away from the shoreline. He had watched as the elderly man clutched at his throat and fell to the ground, unseen by his people.

Joe had only taken basic first aid, but the chief's body language looked exactly like what his instructor had described as the universal gesture that meant "I'm choking." Before Joe had time to think, he had run to the back of the boat and launched himself into the water. Only as he pushed against the weight of the water and marched onto the sand did the situation move into his conscious mind.

To his right, the Huapi jabbed their spears and made obnoxious noises. He'd never seen the gestures or heard the sounds before, but their meaning was clear, too. They did not like the tourists, not at all, and they wanted them to leave. The Huapi men performed these gestures with such passion they didn't notice Joe bolting around behind them.

He found the chief rolling in the sand, clutching his throat, his tanned face turning a sickly purple. Joe helped him up and flung his arms about the larger man's belly. The Huapi man flailed, confused and terrified. Joe placed his fist below the chief's sternum and pulled in and up.

Again. Again. Again.

Maubombo gave up all resistance. He could feel his eyes slipping beyond his control, rolling skyward as his lungs crushed his insides, begging for air. Lightning shot through his brain, leaving an afterimage of pounding agony on the inside of his skull. Someone was trying to help him, but the chief had given up. He decided it was best to die now and end this pain.

6

"Come on!" Joe growled, thrusting again.

He had only performed the maneuver once, and that was on an inflatable doll. Thrusting into an actual human belly was incredibly tiring.

"Come on, you big oaf!" Joe gasped. The chief was fading from consciousness, his legs buckling. Joe was concentrating on holding him up, barely aware that the clearing had fallen silent.

The Huapi surrounded them, their eyes distrusting, angry. Cameras continued to flash from the rocking boat beyond.

Joe ignored the crowd closing around him, pulling in harder on the chief's abdomen. "Come on," he mumbled. "Wherever you are, come back!" The natives raised their spears and stepped forward cautiously.

The tour guide, her clothes dripping wet, pushed through the circle, chattering in Huapi. The angry men yelled back at her, spears still raised.

"I'm telling them you're helping," she said, gasping for breath.

"Thanks," Joe grunted, thrusting again.

She spoke again in Huapi. The circle closed in.

"What are they saying?" Joe gasped.

"If he dies, we both die."

Joe thrust again, panting, exhausted. The Huapi were now yelling at each other.

"And," Nina added, "they are arguing over whether to just kill us now. They don't trust you. Or me."

Joe ignored her. "Come on!" he yelled, and thrust.

"Come on!" Thrust.

"Puke, you big-" Thrust.

The chief retched, the bark shooting out of his mouth. He sputtered to life like a motorcycle kicked awake, broke free of Joe's grasp and fell face first into the sand. Joe fell backwards, panting, spear-tips hovering inches from his face. Nina spoke faster and faster, hands out, palms forward.

The chief was still vomiting as the younger Huapi helped him up. The other Huapi men kept Joe and Nina surrounded. They huddled together under the jagged points. The chief's eyes were glazed over, but they held a wily gleam as well. His mouth turned up and he coughed a chuckle. He winced in pain, spittle hanging from his lips as he laughed.

The Huapi lowered their spears and slapped Joe on his back. Nina stared at him, her eyes wide.

"You did it," she said, smiling.

"I did it," he gasped.

"You did it," she laughed.

"We did it. They would have killed me. You saved my life."

"Only because you saved his."

"Excuse me a moment," Joe said, breaking away from the Huapi.

He slowly walked to the edge of the river, his back to them all. The chaos of the tour boat quieted as everyone onboard watched him wade into the water.

His scream began softly, low, like a lion roaring. He lifted his head to face the sky, arms raised above as far as they could stretch.

"I did it!" he yelled. He turned, his face bright red. "Waaaahooooo!"

Nina echoed his victory whoop and threw her arms around him in a huge hug.

The Huapi rushed to meet them, hugging, mobbing, chanting, everyone celebrating that death had been cheated.

"We did it!" Nina and Joe yelled as they were lifted high on the Huapi men's shoulders.

"And I don't even know your name!" Joe yelled to her.

Nina looked back as they were carried into the jungle. The boat passengers were clapping wildly. Paulo gunned the engine, carrying them away down the river.

Nina and Joe bounced through the dark forest, riding high on song and rhythm, colors of fruits and flowers spilling around them against a backdrop of deep black green.

From on top of the Huapi men's shoulders, they shouted to each other.

"I'm Nina!" she called out, ducking under a branch.

"Joe!"

"Nice to meet you!"

"Same here!"

"Where are we going?"

"I don't know! I guess to their village."

"Is that good?" he asked half-seriously. "We're not going to be cooked and eaten, are we?"

She smiled. "The Huapi aren't cannibals anymore. They stopped that centuries ago. I think."

He tried to reply, but the words bounced out of him as they were carried into the dark green.

Part 2

1

Just when Joe felt as if his stomach was going to spring up out of his mouth, he and his bearers passed over a creek and into the center of a cluster of huts, roofed with the large leaves of the forest. He and Nina were set down in the middle of the Huapi village.

The men scattered, calling out, while the chief crushed both Nina and Joe in a bear hug. The rest of the village came running, joining in the celebration. Men, women and children jumped in place, raising their fists and hooting in a deep rhythmic chant. The chief walked among them, smiling, touching their faces.

"Joe Vera," Joe said, extending his hand to Nina.

"Nina Vasquez," she replied, shaking his hand.

They both spun in a circle, admiring the excited scene around them, the pulsating song, the pounding drums, the dancing everywhere.

"It sounds like a heartbeat," Joe said.

"It does."

"What does it mean?"

"I speak their language, but I don't know everything about the Huapi," Nina said. "We're both in new territory here. We'll have to rely on instinct."

"Okay. So what's your instinct tell you now?"

"All good news. Obviously this is a celebration. They're running off to get everyone to come see us. We're heroes. Well, you are."

"Don't count yourself out. You kept them from killing me."

"I'm a little surprised. I thought you were dead meat."

"Now you tell me. So, how big is this tribe?"

"By most counts, there's only about one hundred left."

"That's all?"

"That's it. And shrinking every year."

"Did you see where the chief went?"

"Here he comes now."

The throng parted and quieted as the chief strode toward Joe and Nina, still occasionally coughing roughly. He was followed by a woman and a surly young man whom Joe recognized as one who had been jabbing a spear at him. The young man glared as the chief embraced Joe in another rib-cracking bear hug and began speaking to him.

"Uh, thanks," Joe said. He leaned toward Nina, "What's he saying? Why is he laughing?"

Nina translated. "He's saying, 'Thank you, great hero. You are exceptional for a white man.'"

Joe laughed back. "Thanks. I try." Nina interpreted his words for the chief.

"And this is his wife, Yuala, and his son, Ndiko. They offer their thanks for saving his life."

"Can you repeat the son's name? How do you say it?"

"En-dee-koh, but you barely pronounce the N."

"He looks like he wants to kill me."

The young man glared at Joe as the chief's wife clasped Joe's hands and squeezed hard. Tears ran down her wrinkled bronze face.

Joe looked to Nina. "What should I say? I've never saved someone's life before. Hey, what are you saying?"

"I told him you did what any human would do. I hope you don't mind."

The chief chuckled while pinching Joe's cheek. Joe stepped back, holding his face. "What the hell?"

"He said your modesty is surprising and he wanted to make sure you were white. He said his tribe didn't save him. Only your magic did."

"I'm not a magician," Joe said.

Nina didn't translate that. There was too much going on, too many people talking at once, as the rest of the tribe crowded in, dancing and hooting. Joe kept colliding with people as the mob shifted, but the chief's wife clung to him through it all, almost causing him to lose his balance. She kept talking, her mouth trembling.

"Yuala appreciates what you've done," Nina translated. "She loves her husband despite his foolishness, she wants you to thanks you for saving him."

Joe smiled back at the old Huapi woman. She released him to wipe at her tears. He could feel his own eyes filling up.

The chief grabbed the shoulder of the angry young man behind him and pulled him forward.

"And this," Nina interpreted, "is Ndiko. The Chief's son."

Ndiko sneered at Joe, then reached up to pinch Joe's cheek like his father had done. Fingernails dug in and scratched. Joe pulled back.

"Damn it!"

Ndiko smirked and growled something.

Nina explained. "He says you're still white."

"That hurt."

The chief shoved his son back, and turned to embrace Joe yet again. This time he held him at a distance while clasping his shoulders and talking.

"I am Maubombo," Nina translated, "Chief of the Huapi people. Thank you for saving my life. You are a hero and we will celebrate!"

The tribe began to whoop as the Chief yelled out to them. Nina continued translating, "We will celebrate the hero and his wife!"

Nina and Joe looked at each other, laughing. "Wife?"

The crowd around them splintered, running into the forest, disappearing into the huts. Some returned with bowls of fruit, some with jugs filled with a pungent wine-like drink. Others began a bonfire and the rest swarmed over Nina and Joe, touching them, hugging them, pinching their cheeks and patting their heads.

"Let's party!" Nina yelled.

2

As the sun set, the celebration increased its intensity, the chanting growing louder, the dancing more furious. The Huapi kept slapping Joe and Nina on the back while the two drank from constantly refilled jugs. They drank past the buzz, past being drunk, past when their eyes were floating. Fruit of every color was laid before them, and meat from a forest creature cooked on the fire. All the while, they were surrounded by vigorous activity, singing and drumming from young and old, man and woman.

The entire forest seemed to throb with excitement.

"I always dreamed of being a hero," Joe said.

Nina nodded agreement as she chewed a small piece of bark.

Joe continued. "I just never knew it would happen at a rave. In the jungle. In South America."

"It's even better that it's among the Huapi," Nina said. "They're not always friendly with outsiders. It took me forever to teach myself the language."

"So how exactly did you come to be here?"

"My parents moved our whole family to the USA when I was ten. I came back during a trip for college, fell in love with the place and never went back."

"So, you're Palaguan."

"Full-blooded. But you stay around here long enough and even your pasty skin will darken. The sun bakes everyone a Palaguan bronze."

"And the Huapi are even darker than you."

"They even call us Palaguans pales."

"Your home is beautiful," Joe said, looking around the jungle.

"This part of it, anyway."

Before she could say more, they were lifted to their feet and forced to take part in the dancing. Soon, Nina and Joe were joined with the tribe, their bare feet pounding the dirt in time with the drummers.

A community pipe was passed to them and they smoked it deeply, agreeing that whatever it was, it was far better than the best pot they had ever toked. They spun around dancing and the stars spun with them.

3

Joe woke up in the dark, an intense headache gripping his skull. He groaned.

He realized he was sleeping on the ground, directly on the packed earth, in a Huapi hut. His whole body was sore. Someone stirred next to him. It startled him, but in his mellow state he didn't jump. A woman moaned.

"Nina?"

"It's me."

"Just checking," Joe said, leaning back to go to sleep. She rolled toward him, half on him, her hands sliding clumsily over his chest.

"Nina, what are you doing?"

"After what you did, you deserve this."

"I didn't save his life to get laid."

"And I didn't save yours for the same reason. I just can't think too straight and I don't care. Let's celebrate right."

"But... but... you don't have to."

"I know. I want to."

"But... but..."

"Shh..."

"Well... okay."

4

A rough hand was touching Joe's face. He tried to speak, but a palm pressed over his lips.

"Shh..." a voice said in the dark, and the hand lifted.

"Not again, you wild woman," Joe said. "You already wore me out." He tried to roll over, but rough hands pulled him back. They were not a woman's hands.

He yelped, and the heavy palm pressed down on his mouth again.

His eyes adjusted to the weak light.

The chief was kneeling over him.

Joe leapt to his feet, his head brushing the roof of the hut.

"Don't tell me I slept with you."

The chief tilted his head, his forehead wrinkled.

Nina moaned nearby in the dark.

"Nina! Nina!" Joe hissed. "Oh, thank God! We had sex, right?"

"Thanks a lot. I guess it wasn't too memorable, huh?"

"No I don't mean. Oh, thank God it was you. We've got a visitor."

"What?"

She lifted herself and spun around.

The chief smiled broadly, pushing his palms toward the earth, signaling quiet. Joe and Nina nodded their understanding. The chief whispered to Nina in Huapi.

"He wants us to follow," she said. The chief added something else.

"And be extremely quiet about it," Nina said.

"Where are we going?" Joe whispered.

The chief answered.

"Trust him. You'll like it," Nina said, shrugging.

They crept through the village. Dozens of Huapi were sleeping on the ground. Some on their backs, some curled together. The silent crowd's calm breathing created an atmosphere of relaxation. The golden pre-dawn sky still had not woken them, proof of their party's magnitude.

The chief led them through the jungle, pushing his way through the growth. He kept looking over his shoulder, smiling and beckoning. Joe's feet hurt and Nina was soon limping, but the herbs and bark they had consumed continued to swirl through their blood, slowing time and making the trip bearable.

Soon they were squeezing between wet rocks, penetrating the mountainside into almost complete darkness. The chief whispered back to them.

"He says we're almost there," Nina said.

"Good. This is starting to get tight," Joe grunted as he scraped through yet another small stone passage.

They crawled down over damp moss, pushing deep into the earth. Ahead, light shimmered around a corner.

"What is it?" Joe asked. "An underground stream?"

The chief reached the end of the tunnel, then stopped. Beyond him, colored light flickered on the cave wall. He gestured with his hands, indicating they were to walk past him and look.

They turned the corner and were dumbstruck, their mouths dropping open.

5

Though the cave was absent sunlight, they could easily see. Light emanated from a translucent layer of crystal lining the cavern's interior. Inside the semi-transparent layer, colors exploded and shone outward, like a hundred tiny prisms gently rotating as they shot color into the air.

Shades swirled and pulsated inside the walls, floor and ceiling endlessly. When the random spots happened to synchronize, they formed a temporary swath of one color, then splintered into a thousand tiny abstract shapes. The pulsating would join again, then separate once more. Every basic color of the rainbow was represented.

Joe and Nina stood staring, bold hues passing across their faces like people looking skyward at a fireworks show. Their mouths gaped as they stood in silent astonishment for several minutes. The chief smiled at them. A peaceful trickle of water dripped on the translucent floor.

"My God!" Nina finally cried.

"What is this?" Joe whispered, sounding to himself like he was afraid. "I've never seen anything like it. Nothing in person, nothing on television, nothing that I've ever heard of comes close to this. It's the aurora borealis caught in glass."

"A million tiny rainbows are caught inside the crystal. Only they don't need light passing through them to create color. This is coming from inside."

"It's like we're inside a natural lava lamp."

The chief smiled, walking aimlessly, holding his hand out, catching color in his palm. He watched their reaction with pride.

"Amazing," Nina said.

"We're not still high, are we?" Joe asked.

She wiped her eyes. "I've never seen anything so beautiful."

Joe choked up as well. "Me either. I- I'm in awe."

They stumbled about, absently brushing their fingers through the colored mist.

"What is it?" Joe spoke, touching the crystal that clung to the wall. "Is it alive?"

"I don't think so. This is rock. It's actually in the rock. Look! Even the ones we're standing on. Like a- like a- natural disco floor."

"Something like that." He kneeled to touch the cave's floor. Colors danced across his fingertips. "It's beyond beautiful," he whispered. "I'm at a loss for words. It's magic. A miracle."

The chief said something in Huapi to Nina.

"It's a gift from the gods, he says."

"If anything ever was, this is."

The chief spoke again. Nina answered. They talked while Joe ignored them, transfixed by the twinkling colors in the floor.

"Thank you," she said, slowly, articulated.

The chief approached Joe, clasped his shoulder and stared into his eyes. Red, blue, then purple and yellow crossed over their faces, the random shapes of vibrant clouds passing.

"Thank you," the chief said in English to Joe. He started to speak again but turned to Nina before turning to Nina.

"For saving," she said.

"For saving," the chief repeated, facing Joe again.

"My life."

"My life," the chief said, smiling.

Joe smiled and gasped to breathe, assaulted by another one of the chief's lung-crunching hugs.

"How do I say 'You're welcome, and thank you' back?" Joe asked Nina when he was released.

Nina told him.

Joe stared at the chief seriously and spoke the words as he had heard them from Nina, meeting the chief's eyes.

"You found welcome from toenail."

They all laughed.

The chief turned and picked up a fragment of the crystal that fit in his palm. The pieces lay strewn about across the cave floor, the result of a mass of the crystal cracking off from the cave wall, falling and shattering.

The chief clutched the crystal in his hand. Rainbows launched out from between his fingers. He guided the colors about the cave walls in a psychedelic dance. He then handed it to Joe, speaking.

Nina interpreted. "A gift. To you."

"I'm honored," Joe said, choking back tears, taking the crystal with two hands.

The chief grinned and hugged them both, his eyes watering. "Thank you," he said again in English. Then he said something in Huapi.

Nina explained to Joe. "He said, 'Thank you for allowing me to see this again.'"

They would have stayed forever, but their stomachs growled, becoming more insistent until their hunger could no longer be ignored.

The chief led them outside.

As they emerged from the cave, someone leapt down from a tree in front of them, startling them.

It was Ndiko, the chief's son. Face tense, he confronted his father.

"Father! What are you doing?" Ndiko yelled, banging the butt of his spear on the ground. He pointed at Joe and Nina.

"Where did this come from?"

"I think we've got a problem," Joe said, standing back inside the cave entrance. Nina stood with him, translating.

"I am rewarding those who saved my life," Maubombo answered, puffing his chest out, strutting forward.

"We just had a celebration for them," his son yelled. "There is no need to bring them here."

Maubombo slapped him. "I am the chief and you will learn respect."

Ndiko spun his spear behind his father's knees and knocked him father to the ground. He pointed the unsharpened end at his chest.

"You are the one who disrespects our land!"

Joe stepped back into the cave entrance, shoving the crystal in his pocket.

"What should we do? Should I return the crystal?"

Nina hesitated.

The chief coughed, cursing at his son from the ground, "You will respect me and my decisions."

"Father, this is a gift from the gods. To the Huapi. And you share it with the pales?"

"This white one saved my life. When I was dying, he came. You didn't!"

"Best to just stay back for now," Nina whispered.

"I was hoping you'd say that," Joe said, "since he's the one with the spear."

The son towered over his father. "I was protecting you! Who knew he was working white-man magic?" Ndiko turned the spear point on Joe.

"I don't want to cause trouble," Joe said, holding the crystal shard out palm up. Nina stepped out from behind Joe, quickly translating.

"Now, white man, you insult me?" the chief asked Joe as he struggled to his feet.

"No insult is intended," Joe responded with Nina's help. "I simply want to keep peace in your village, your family."

Maubombo thundered, "All of you must stop defying my will!" He jabbed his finger at Joe. "Take the crystal, or I will be insulted."

"But, father!" Ndiko yelled.

"Silence. It is only a tiny piece! One small piece!"

"You betray us more than the white man," Ndiko mumbled, then turned and ran into the dense forest.

The three walked back to the village through the orange sunrise. The quiet aftermath of the argument kept them silent. The village was awakening; those already up were cooking an oatmeal-like substance over a flame. The chief snapped off small pieces of bark from a vine-strangled tree and handed them to Nina and Joe for chewing.

"No more bark for me," the chief chuckled.

Joe frowned, looking into his pocket where colors danced in the dark.

"Should I give the crystal back?" he asked Nina. "Last chance."

"Just keep it quiet. We've already caused enough trouble."

7

As the Huapi went about their daily routines of gathering food and preparing to hunt, Yuala, the chief's wife, brought Nina and Joe bowls of an oatmeal-like breakfast. They thanked her and ate in silence, both wincing while they swallowed the drab chewy mush.

Nina watched Yuala interact with Chief Maubombo. She could tell his wife knew something was wrong, but was keeping up her lively personality in front of the guests.

"Can you tell her this is very good?" Joe said.

Nina translated for Yuala who nodded thanks and squeezed out a smile but said nothing.

A boat's motor and horn sounded in the distance. The Huapi looked up, startled.

"That would be Paulo," Nina said, standing.

"We should go," she told Maubombo.

He opened his arms wide.

"My friends, my friends," he said. "You are welcome back here any time."

Once more, he crushed them in his arms. The Huapi made a line for them to pass, smiling as they went by, pinching their cheeks, patting their hands. It took over a half-hour to get to the end of the line.

Ndiko was not present to say goodbye.

Nina and Joe smiled and headed down the path to the river, led by a silent Huapi guide.

Paulo had run the boat aground where he had left them. They could see the ship's mud-speckled white hull through the trees.

"Down that way will take you out to the river," the guide said to Nina, mumbling in Huapi. He ducked back into the jungle so quickly, he seemed to vanish.

"Hey, Boss!" Paulo said, calling from the boat as Joe and Nina emerged.

They sat in the cabin of the empty tour boat as Paulo started the engine and steered them back to Palagua City port.

Nina and Joe stared at the floor, exhausted, silent.

"So, what happened?" Paulo asked.

"You won't believe it," Nina answered.

"Must have been some party."

"It was," Joe said.

Nina turned to him.

"Do you realize the honor you've experienced?"

He patted the rock in his pocket. "I'm still absorbing it."

"They usually avoid white people. It's extremely rare for them to speak to any of us, unless they're looking for the nearby mission to convert to Christianity and leave the tribe."

"Are you going to share your story with me?" Paulo asked.

"In a bit," Nina answered. "It's just a lot to absorb. We're not being rude. Maybe you should go first. Anything exciting happen while I was gone?"

"Nothing new. Lots of drunk tourists. For the remaining tours, I had to drive them around in circles in the bay, and make up some history. The few who paid attention weren't happy. I'm not nearly as good as you. But the drunks didn't care. They never do."

"That's the truth."

"Oh, and more rebel talk on the radio. Some mayor in the north was assassinated. The Palaguan Revolutionary Movement took responsibility. They're going to take over the world, you know, build a socialist heaven. Same old same old."

They rode a while without talking, the water splashing hard against the boat, overpowering any conversation. The sun was high and the heat too strong for much talking. Joe kept his hand clamped around the small crystal in his pocket. He imagined the rainbow that burst from within dancing in his palm.

As they neared the shade of the jungle surrounding the marina, he tapped Paulo on the shoulder.

"Look. Check this out," he said, pulling the crystal from his pocket.

"What is that?" Paulo said. "That's wild. What is it?"

The boat swerved dangerously toward the dock.

"Watch out!" Nina yelled.

Paulo swung the boat back on course and stared again at Joe's crystal.

"It's like the colors are shooting out of it. That's amazing. I've never seen anything like that before. It's beautiful. Gorgeous. Where did you get it?"

"The chief gave it to me. Said it was a gift from their gods and he wanted to thank me. It caused a bit of controversy with his son."

"Nice souvenir," Paulo chuckled. "Much better than the junk they sell in Palagua City. I'll pay you for it."

Joe laughed.

"I'm serious."

"It's not for sale."

"Too bad. I bet you could make a lot."

8

When the loudspeaker announced Joe's flight, he and Nina rose at the same time.

"So, did you enjoy your trip?" she asked.

"I wanted have a unique adventure. I got a lot more than I expected."

"Well, your family will be glad to have you back."

"Family? We're scattered all over. Some good friends are what I call my family. You?"

"Just me down here. I spend most of my time with Paulo, but that's strictly business."

"Just you and the Huapi."

"I've always been fascinated by the indigenous peoples. The Huapi are just one of many. They just happen to be the ones closest to Palagua City marina. They're also the smallest. And another interesting fact-"

The loudspeaker announced Joe's flight again.

"Don't get me started," Nina said. "I'll never stop talking."

"Nice people, those Huapi," Joe said. "Very nice people. I'll never forget them." He tapped his pocket where the crystal sparkled colorfully.

"I'm jealous of your prize," Nina said, "But thanks for getting me closer to them."

"Thanks for saving my life by talking them down."

She laughed. They kissed awkwardly. She squeezed his hand.

"Stay in touch," he said. "I need you to keep my boring life interesting."

"A postcard every day," she said.

They both smiled. He waved and left.

Part 3

1

Teri Young tore open her front door and squealed. Joe Vera stumbled as she half-tackled, half-hugged him, forcing him backwards down the cement steps that led to her townhome's entrance.

"Teri, please," Joe gasped. "You're going to kill me."

She released him. "I'm sorry! I'm just so excited. So glad you're back. How are you? How was it? Look at you! You've lost so much weight! You look great! Tan, too!" She kissed him carefully on the cheek before backing away.

"You look good, too," he said.

"Thanks."

"So. What did I miss?"

"Oh, nothing. Nothing at all. You're the one who went on the adventure. You tell us how it went!"

"Speaking of, how is he?"

"Not great. But not bad. More tests, more chemo, you know. Same sickness." Her cheerful face wilted just a little.

"Did his father show up?"

"Oh, please."

"I'm sorry."

"Sorry? Forget it. Save that for later. Come on in. Let's hear all about your trip. He'll be glad to see you. You're the best medicine he's got."

Joe smiled, kissed her on the cheek and stepped by, being sure not to brush against her.

"Hey, Ace," he yelled into the living room.

Billy Young raised his skinny pre-teen arms above his bandana-covered head. He ran to Joe.

"Joe!" They hugged tightly.

"So what have you been up to?" Joe asked.

"No," Billy said. "You first!"

Joe sat down and told them.

He shared the whole story of his wanderings around Palagua, ending with the boat tour. Billy's eyes were huge the whole time. The boy's amazement unnerved Joe because it seemed a little like worship, especially when Joe told of saving the Chief's life. Joe carefully left out the detail about the crystal he took home. He talked for hours, showed his pictures and answered frantic questions. Teri sat by, getting them drinks, silently listening and smiling at her son.

When he finished he turned to Billy.

"Your turn, kid. What have you been up to?"

"Reading. Reading about mythology."

"Who's your favorite? I always liked Perseus. I think. Isn't that the guy who killed Medusa?"

"He's okay. But I like Hercules best."

"Hercules? Why?"

"The twelve labors. Each one took a different skill, they were like puzzles. All the other heroes just killed stuff. At least Herc had to use his brain, too."

"Good point."

"Herc was a hero like you. You saved the chief!"

Joe laughed. "I just did the right thing, that's all. I'm no match for Herc."

"I guess."

"You guess? He did twelve labors, right? I can barely keep one job."

"Yeah, but you're cool."

"You're cool, too."

"I guess."

"You guess?" Joe leaned forward and started tickling Billy. The boy screeched as they tumbled to the floor, wrestling. Billy's bandana slipped loose from his bald head. Teri sat back and laughed nearly to the point of crying.

A small wrapped package tumbled from Joe's pocket and rolled across the rug.

"What's that?" he pointed behind Billy to where the bundle had fallen.

"The oldest trick in the book, that's what," Billy said. They were both on their knees, grappling. He lunged at Joe.

"No, really."

"Mom?" Billy said, keeping an eye on Joe, slapping his hands away. "Is he lying?"

"No. There's really a present on the floor."

Billy turned quickly and picked it up.

"A little present for you from Palagua," Joe said.

Billy tore off the wrapping paper and opened the box. The multicolored beams shot out to the ceiling. Billy reached in and gasped, pulling out the crystal.

All three of them were silent as Billy spun around, spraying the room with prismatic colors. Transfixed, they watched the rainbows slide across the walls.

Billy screeched enthusiastically.

"Awesome! Look at it! Is this the one you talked about?"

"A gift direct from Maubombo," Joe said, "Chief of the Huapi tribe in the heart of Palaguan rainforest."

"Oh, my God, it's beautiful," Teri said.

"Look at the colors!" Billy yelled. He held the crystal high above his head. Light glowed inside his fist.

"It's like that fish we saw on TV, the one that shines in the dark parts of the ocean," Teri said. "The bio-lumin-something."

"Bio-luminescence," Billy said. "Is that what it is, Joe?"

"I don't know. I have no idea. You're the smart one, kid."

"What do you say, Billy?" Teri asked.

"Thanks, Joe! Thank you."

The boy hugged him close, turning his head to the side, and crushing his tiny frame into Joe's chest with all his might. Joe winked over his head at Teri.

"And I got this for you," Joe said to her, handing her a necklace made of pale blue-pink shells. "Hand-made by the Huapi women."

"It's beautiful," Teri said, taking it from him, barely looking at it. She was staring, mesmerized by the crystal's colors dancing in the air.

* * *

Billy eventually fell asleep on the couch, still gripping the crystal. Color twinkled between his fingers.

Joe and Teri slipped away to the kitchen to sip coffee.

"So. Tell me about this tour guide lady," Teri said.

"Oh, her? Nothing serious. I shouldn't even have mentioned her."

"Just wondering, that's all."

"We're friends, just like you and I. Only not as strong, of course. I just met her. And she and I don't have a history."

"Oh, I know," Teri said. "She couldn't build a history like ours in a hundred years."

Joe laughed. "Nina was just someone I met in a bizarre situation. If I really got to know her, she's probably a bitch."

"Probably." Teri smiled.

They sat in silence for a minute. Teri looked away from him.

"He's doing worse," she whispered.

"He seems a little different. Maybe weaker. Slower."

"His tests show the cancer is growing. Nothing drastic right now, but it means more medicine to fight it off. It's like a monster, creeping slowly..."

Slowly but surely, she left unsaid.

Joe simply nodded and squeezed the top of her hand. She breathed in and exhaled deeply, her eyes closed.

A single tear snuck out between her eyelashes. Joe wiped it away.

"He'll be all right," he said.

2

Maubombo stared at the sunset from the south side of the mountain that acted as a natural divider between Palagua City and the Huapi village. He sat with his arm around his wife. Since his visit to the verge of death, he had demanded that his family be together as much as possible.

"Where's my son?" he said.

"Late again," Yuala sighed.

"I don't know what he's waiting for. The evening is always so beautiful. We never know how much time we have."

Ndiko stepped from the darkness of the forest. Without a word, he sat down on a rock, rested his chin in his hand and glared at the ground.

"What is it?" his mother asked. "You've been moody for days. Is it a girl?" There was a hopeful tone to her question.

"Father should never have given the gift of the gods to a white man." Ndiko said, not looking up.

"Oh, this again," Yuala moaned. "But the white man's boats no longer come around. Is that not a gift? Since your father showed his generosity, they no longer stink up our homes with smoke. They are not here anymore to stare or wake us up."

"That's because the white woman has told them not to come by anymore."

"If that is true, she did that because of your father's kindness."

"You dare say the gods are not all-powerful?" Maubombo said. "If they were angry with me, I would be punished. Do you think they would let me see this gorgeous sunset every day?"

"I'm saying-"

"One day, son," Maubombo said, "you will learn that leading a tribe is not easy."

"I would never give away the gift from the gods."

"Maybe you would if someone saved your life."

"It was the whites who put you in danger! No white could ever give me anything. I have all I need in the forest."

"You proud fool."

Ndiko rose and strode to the edge of the jungle. "I'm not coming to this evening gathering anymore." He vanished into the green.

Maubombo sat in silence, pouting. Finally he spoke. "What's wrong with that boy?"

Yuala leaned into her husband and rubbed his tense back and shoulders. "He's stubborn," she said, with just the right amount of humor and calm.

"He's like his father."

3

"Mom…"

Teri had just gotten home from work and was barely inside the door when her son called her. She dropped her laptop computer and listened. She could tell something was wrong from the crack and sob in his voice.

"Billy? Where are you?"

She started walking toward the living room, balling her fist.

"Tee Vee," he said, his voice sounding like his nose was stuffed.

"Oh, my God."

Billy was sprawled on the couch, head back, tissues stuffed up his nose. Blood spilled down the front of his shirt. Dirt and sticks clung to his clothes and his cheeks were bruised. Tears left muddy streaks down his cheekbones.

"Hi, Mom," he said, frowning with bloody lips.

"Oh, my baby," she said, running her hand over his thin hair, pulling sticks off his sweatshirt.

"I got in a fight."

"I can see that. Are you hurt?"

"No." He started to sob, clenching his eyes shut. "Not too much."

"Shh. It's okay, baby. Just calm down. Tell me where."

"He- he took the stone."

"The stone?"

Billy snorted again. "The crystal Joe gave me. I brought it to school and…"

"Shh. We'll get it back. Right now, let's clean you up."

* * *

Later that night, Billy went to bed early. When the phone rang Teri answered it quickly.

"Hello?"

"Hello? Is this is the home of Billy Young?"

"Who's calling?"

"My name is Ethan Scherr. You can call me Ethan."

"What is the purpose of this call?"

"Are you Billy's mother?"

"I am."

"Well, it's nice to meet-"

"Tell me what this call is about or I'm hanging up."

"Forgive me. Our sons had a bit of an altercation at school today."

"Oh. You."

"Yes. I'd like to personally bring my boy Cory over to apologize."

Teri was dumbstruck for a moment. "Apologize?" she said.

'What the heck is this?' she thought. 'A 1950s television show? Who brings their kids over to apologize anymore?'

"That's very kind of you, Mr. Scherr, but I'd like to talk it over with my son first."

"Well, if that's how you feel, of course we can wait. I just wanted your boy to get his toy rock thing back as soon as possible."

"I expect Billy's property returned regardless."

"Of course. However, I'd really like to accompany my son there to talk with you and Billy. To express my regrets."

"I will talk to him about it. It's up to him."

"Of course." They exchanged phone numbers.

"I'll call you back," Teri said. She slammed the phone down.

4

"What do you think, kid?" Teri asked Billy as he was getting ready for school the next day.

"I don't know. Tomorrow's Saturday. I want to hang with Joe."

"Does that boy tease you a lot?"

"Not really."

"Billy..."

"Yes."

"And you stood up to him."

"Yes."

"That's my boy."

"But I lost, mom. He kicked my ass. He wanted Joe's crystal. Everyone at school thought it was awesome. They all kept coming up to me," he said, choking a little, "asking if they could see it. Then Cory said 'Give it to me,' and I said 'No' and then…"

Teri ground her teeth. Her heart broke when she saw the disappointment in his eyes.

"It's all right," she said. "The important thing is you stood up to him."

"I guess. But."

"But what?"

Billy's eyes filled with tears again. "I lost the magic stone Joe gave me."

"We're going to get it back, Billy. The only question is, do you want him to come over and apologize?"

"I don't know."

"What his father is making him do is a big thing."

"Yeah."

"Well? Yes or no?"

"Okay."

Damn, she thought, there goes Saturday.

"Okay," she said, "I'll call Mister Scherr and tell him tomorrow morning is okay with us. Just stay away from that Cory jerk today. Tomorrow morning, we'll get it back. I want you up early, cleaned and you'll have taken all your meds, okay?"

He nodded. "Okay."

* * *

Saturday morning, the doorbell rang. Teri checked her look one more time. She had dressed informal but sporty. She wanted Scherr to know what he could never have.

She pulled down the zipper on her tight jogging top and opened the door.

"Damn," she said, "I completely forgot."

"Going somewhere?" Joe asked. "You look... done up."

She zipped her top up an inch.

"It's a long story."

She told him about how Cory Scherr had stolen the crystal. Billy was coming down the stairs when the doorbell rang again.

5

Paulo sat with Nina in the tiny office of her guided tour company.

"See the natural wonders of Palagua!" a poster promised in English and Spanish. Two squeaky fans were of little use against the oppressive heat and humidity. Nina looked at the records again and shook her head.

Paulo addressed her unspoken concern.

"We're getting beat by the other tour companies because we used to go through Huapi territory. We promised them at least a chance to see the natives."

"The other tours don't even know who the Huapi are."

"I know, but they show the tourists something unique. Some of the larger tribes."

"Those tribes are totally assimilated into Palaguan culture. They're paid to put on a show. It's theater. And bad theater at that."

"But it's something."

"We won't go by the Huapi anymore," Nina said.

"It was the only thing that separated us. My small boat got where their yachts couldn't. Now, we're just like the others, chasing caimans and birds, but without the money to sponsor the bad theater. Or to stock stronger alcohol."

"We're not going into the Huapi territory anymore."

"Why?"

"I don't want tourists staring at them like they're in a zoo. They're people."

"They were people before."

"Well, now it's different. Chart another route, okay? We'll be fine. So we make a little less money."

"I like you, Nina. But I'm not driving this boat for free."

"I never said you were. Just do it and stop talking about it. All right? Just do it."

"Sure, no problem," Paulo said, shaking his head.

6

The tall man's wavy grey-black hair was heavily gelled. He smiled a shiny smile as he reached his hand across the doorway. A young boy stood next to him, his head bowed.

Teri shook the older man's hand.

"Miss Young? I'm Ethan Scherr. Nice to meet you."

Joe reached out and over Scherr's son, purposefully knocking the boy on the head with his elbow.

"I'm Joe Vera, friend of the family."

"Nice to meet you, Joe. This is my son, Cory. Say hello, son."

The boy mumbled without looking up. "Hello."

"Say you're sorry."

"I'm sorry."

"Now, where's Billy?" Ethan asked.

"I'm here," Billy said.

Joe and Teri parted to let him through.

Cory refused to look up. He recited his apology as if every word pained him. "Billy, I'm very sorry for what I did. I should be kind to you. I shouldn't have hit you. I'm very sorry."

Billy didn't react until Cory was done. Then he abruptly said, "You have my crystal."

"Oh, yes," Mr. Scherr said. He pulled the rock from his pocket. Rainbow colors twirled up and down his suit. "You wanted this."

Billy stuck out his hand, palm up.

"Where did you get it?" Scherr asked, keeping it out of Billy's reach.

Teri snatched from him and gave it to Billy.

"Thank you for returning it," she said.

"I can't help but be curious where you found it. It seems natural, not a toy."

"It is natural," Joe said.

"Thank you for the apology and thank you for returning what belongs to Billy," Teri cut in. "That was very big of you, Cory. You too, Mr. Scherr. Now, we have to move on." She started to push the door closed.

Ethan blocked it gently with his foot. He held out a business card.

"Here's my card. I'm in sales and I guarantee we can make some money off that crystal."

Joe took the card. "Good thing I didn't tell you where I got it," he said. "You'd go sell them yourself."

Ethan laughed. "A little paranoid? I don't blame you. I have the contacts and you have the knowledge. I'm willing to work with you."

"It's time to go," Teri said, but she could see Joe was curious. Cory shifted uneasily.

"Let's sit down with some lawyers," Scherr said. "Hash out a plan. You get the finder's fee, I get the commission. Deal?" He stuck out his hand.

Joe didn't shake. "I'll be in touch if I'm interested."

"I look forward to it," Ethan replied. "Call me tomorrow. What do you have to lose?"

Teri was still pushing the door. "Thank you both for coming. Have a good night."

"I can see it's time to go," Ethan said, backing away from the door. "Nice meeting you all. Joe, call me. Let's make some money." He turned and walked down the porch steps with his hand on his son's shoulders.

"Thank you and goodbye," Teri called after them, shutting the door firmly.

* * *

Billy ran into the living room, throwing the crystal in the air and catching it, over and over. Rainbows bounced off the walls and ceiling.

"Go take your meds," Teri said. Billy trotted away, still tossing the crystal.

"What do you think?" she asked Joe.

"What do you mean?" he said, fingering the card. "About that guy and his son? Not much. He seems pretty sleazy."

"I mean about the offer he made. To make money selling the crystal."

"That was interesting."

"Yeah."

"He's probably lying."

"Probably."

"But he did say he and I could sit down with some lawyers."

"Mom! Joe! Come on," Billy called. "Let's watch a movie."

"All right, we're coming," Teri said.

Joe looked at the business card one more time before slipping it into his pocket.

The weekend ended and another week began. Teri was preparing dinner on Monday night when the phone rang.

"Hello, Miss Young? Teri? Ethan Scherr here. We met this past weekend. How are you?"

She rolled her eyes. "Good. Yourself?"

"Oh, I'm great. Always great. Listen, did you and your friend Joe have a chance to consider my proposal? I think we've got a great opportunity here."

"Joe and I have talked about it."

"Excellent."

"We have a few concerns. We're still thinking about it. I should tell you, though, the final decision will be his."

"Well, if you just tell me where you found it…"

"He'll call you back if he's interested."

Scherr started to reply, but she hung up.

* * *

Teri found Billy in his bedroom playing a video game with all the lights off. The screen made his nearly bald head shine blue.

The crystal sat by his side on top of the covers, lighting the dark as it cycled through the rainbow's colors. She stared at it for a while, before sitting next to it on bed, making room for it as if it were a living thing.

"So, kid," she said, "does that Cory leave you alone now?"

"Mostly," Billy said, not looking away from his game.

"What do you mean, mostly?"

"Now he just asks me where I got the crystal. I told him from Joe. Then he says, you know what I mean, and I tell him Planet Earth. He looks like he wants to punch me, but he doesn't."

"That's my boy. Don't ever tell him."

"I'm not talking to that asshole."

"Billy! Now you watch your language."

"But it's true."

She paused a moment. "Okay, maybe it's true, but you should still watch your language."

8

Exactly one week after meeting Ethan Scherr, Joe arrived at an upscale restaurant and immediately felt under-dressed. Scherr rose from a table, wearing a full suit and tie, making a noisy show of welcoming him.

"Joe, so glad you made it!"

The conversation began with small talk. Vera could tell Scherr was leading somewhere when he compared the weather to Indonesian rain.

"My wife and I were traveling in Southeast Asia last year," he said. "Have you ever been overseas?"

Joe chuckled. "Why don't we work out a deal instead of playing games?"

Scherr set down his silverware. "A straight-shooter. I like that. I've always admired that. You have that air about you. No B.S."

"I try."

"All right, Mister Vera. I don't mean to seem so persistent, but I am sure that hunk of rock, clay, crystal, stalactite, whatever it is, is going to make us a fortune. I mean, our sons even brawled over it!"

"Billy is not my son."

"The point I'm making is, kids love that crystal. They'll fight for it, which means parents will fight to get it for them. But let's move on to the deal. I want to take that rock and show it around, see if we can sell it."

"Sell it to?"

"Now, Mr. Vera, that's where we need our deal. You've been holding back on where you got it, so I'm afraid I have to hold back on my contacts. You trade me the location of where you found it, and I will tell you who I intend to sell it to. We need to work together. Do we have a deal?"

"I'd want the rock back. It was a gift."

"I don't see that as a problem. Look, why don't we get the lawyers involved?"

"Fine."

"I'll bring my regular guy and someone else for you."

"No thanks, I'll bring my own."

Ethan smiled. "Good man. Cautious. Bordering on paranoid, but smart. I like that. I think we're going to get along fine. Now how about this weather, huh?" Scherr began his small talk again and Joe was fine with that. The aura around the table was changing; a deal had been struck. Two men once adversaries were now partners.

"One second," Joe said, interrupting the light conversation. "How much do you think we stand to make?"

Scherr grinned and his eyes narrowed. "A lot, Joe. A whole lot. I wouldn't be so relentless to talk to you if I thought we would only be making peanuts."

Joe took a deep gulp of the complementary wine and settled into the small talk.

How much was a whole lot? He wondered.

He looked around the restaurant. He still felt under-dressed, but he didn't care so much now.

9

Nina and Paulo's only day away from the guided boat tour business was Sunday. Three weeks ago, she had made her first trip into the Huapi village with a stranger named Joe, both as guests of honor. She felt the need to return. She filled her backpack with snacks and water bottles before heading out on foot, just as the sun was rising into a clear sky.

She had to walk through several miles of city first, among the sprawling ramshackle neighborhoods. One of the things she loved about Palagua City was that there was always something new to see, some place she hadn't been before. This time, instead of wandering within, she was focused more on getting out and reaching the surrounding jungle.

She frowned as she passed the Christian Mission, where the wild green met the urban grey. A statue of some saint stood at the very edge of the forest, beckoning the natives out.

Nina continued on, crashing into the foliage, following a trail that, in the eyes of the Palaguan government, passed for a recreational area. She breathed in the deep, moist darkness. Sweat covered her body in a thin film, but the living air of the rainforest rejuvenated her.

As she reached the end of the trail, she snapped a thick branch from a tree, using it as a make-shift machete to hack her way through the growth. She hacked and hacked until she was soaking with sweat. She stopped several times to rest before continuing.

At last she came to the Huapi village.

From her secluded spot, she watched. Children ran freely among the thatched huts. Men were cooking the fish and small mammals they had found on their hunt. Women were laying out the fruit they had gathered.

She pondered why she liked the Huapi, and realized it was because their culture was satisfied with what it was. It wasn't idyllic, because Palagua City was nearby, the noise and smell of urban life occasionally wafting through the village. It wasn't innocent, because the mission was nearby, accepting any willing Huapi converts.

She liked them because it was just a simple life, and in that simplicity was its beauty. People did their chores to stay alive and when they were done, they played with the children or relaxed or chewed bark or smoked or danced. There wasn't much more to it than that, and that was all anyone really needed.

Nina gently pushed her way through the growth into the village.

She walked in, greeting them in Huapi. This startled them for a moment until Yuala, the chief's wife, rushed up to her and gave her an enthusiastic hug.

"Where did this come from?" she said. "Hello, beautiful lady. Welcome back."

"Thank you," Nina said. "I'm glad you recognized me. I think I gave the others a scare. I just wanted to visit again and say hello."

"Take your seat, then! You are always welcome! Maubombo!" Yuala called. Her husband emerged from a group of men arguing around the cooking of meat. When he saw Nina, he rushed across the clearing and nearly knocked her over as he hugged her, smiling his huge broad smile.

He laughed. "Welcome back, my daughter! When the boats stopped coming I thought I would never see you again."

She blushed. "The boats won't be back. I don't want them to disturb your people anymore."

"You have that kind of power? Or is your husband a chief?"

"I say where the boat goes."

Maubombo found that hilarious. His laughter boomed through the village.

"Where is your son?" Nina asked.

"Oh, just sulking somewhere," Yuala said. "He's not often with us for dinner. He likes to roam around the jungle alone."

Nina nodded her understanding. "Please tell him I said hello."

"If I see him, I will. For now, let's eat."

They sat Nina among the women from the tribe. They ate and talked until the stars rose.

Nina realized this simple life was what she had wanted, why she had moved to Palagua from the United States. They invited her to stay the night, but she declined.

She left after several dozen hugs from Yuala and Maubombo.

The good time lifted her spirit and the natural food gave her the energy to begin the walk back to her apartment with less effort than she expected. She fantasized about one day staying with the Huapi forever, but for now, the habit of preparing for Monday morning work was in her blood, pulling her back. She waved goodbye and smiled as she began the journey back toward the city.

Hidden in the jungle's high branches, Ndiko watched her leave.

Part 4

1

Joe was alone with his lawyer.

Sheldon Mora's office was as quiet as a library and filled with as many books. The chairs, desk and shelves were made of dark wood. Sheldon's hair was peppered gray, nearly white on his sideburns. His suit was dark blue with pinstripes. Joe suspected his entire appearance was designed to instill confidence and just a little bit of intimidation in his clients. It was working.

"Here's the situation," Joe said, feeling under-dressed again and vowing to buy an expensive suit. "There are people living on the land where this crystal is. I'm concerned that if I tell anyone where it is, these people will be displaced and their land polluted. I'm not even sure I should be saying this much."

"Yes. Yes," Sheldon said, nodding, his deep voice resonating with concern. "It's certainly understandable."

"So, how do I prevent any trouble? I want to make sure this is done right, with their permission or no deal."

"All right," Sheldon said. "Very noble of you. Let me float a question by you. What would you like to see in the contract that would put your mind at ease? Pretend you can have anything you want. Say it."

"I'd like to see something that says any use of the land must be cleared by the people who own it, who are living on the land, and they will benefit from the profits. That's what I want."

"Then that's what we'll ask for," Sheldon said, taking notes.

* * *

Joe's head was spinning. He'd taken two days off from work to meet with lawyers and discuss deals with Ethan Scherr. The concentration necessary to keep the secret of the crystal's source made his head throb. They discussed percentages endlessly, and while he was a key part of the deal, he felt his contribution to the entire scheme was small and shrinking. All he had to offer were a few simple words: the name of a nation, the name of a tribe, all the descriptions he could remember.

When they started discussing dollar amounts in the millions, Joe could feel his heart race.

"Poker face," he chanted inside his mind. "Poker face, poker face," he silently repeated as he bit his tongue to keep from screaming with joy.

At the end of the day, his lawyer Sheldon said, "I think we're very close to a deal with your friend Ethan and his lawyer. That wasn't too difficult, was it?"

"No," Joe said, "the toughest part happens tonight."

* * *

"Hey!" Joe bellowed as he crashed through the front door carrying several wrapped packages.

"What is this? Christmas?" Teri asked as he handed her a small present.

"Sort of."

Billy bounded down the stairs.

"Check it out," he squealed as Joe tossed him a package. The boy caught it and threw himself on the couch.

"Joe, look what I made!" Billy lifted the crystal from around his neck, showing off a necklace made from patiently twisted twine and wire. Colors shooting from the crystal formed rainbows on Billy's tiny chest.

"That's awesome," Joe said, his heart pounding, his tongue drying.

"Can I open this?" Billy asked, focusing on his gift.

"First, what do you say?" Teri reminded.

"Thank you, Joe."

"No problem, Ace. Now open it."

Billy tore the wrapping off. "Aw, cool! Classic tales of Mythology, the twelve-chapter graphic novel collection! One for each labor of Hercules! Awesome!"

"And you?" Joe said to Teri.

She opened her box slowly and pulled out an intricately folded gift certificate. "Good for a free hot stone massage! Oh, I could use this," she said, clutching the coupon to her chest. "I need this big-time."

Joe smiled.

"So, what's the occasion?" Teri asked.

"Can I have more presents?" Billy said.

"Wait a minute, let him explain."

"It's like this," Joe began, breathing deeply. "I sat down with Mister Scherr today, and some lawyers."

"You were with Cory the Asshole's dad?" Billy asked, his eyebrows crinkling with suspicion.

"Language," Teri chided.

"Yes, I was with Cory the Asshole's dad," Joe continued, grinning at Teri, who frowned. "We met with some lawyers and worked out a deal. He's going to see if anyone wants to harvest the crystal and get some money. Lots of money. My end of the deal is,

I have to tell them where we found it. After that, Mister Scherr and I split our portion of the profits in half. I keep some of that and a little bit goes to my lawyer."

"Awesome," Billy said.

"Joe, that is just great," Teri cheered.

"Well, that all depends," Joe said, "on if they can market the crystal. They expect they can and that it will be a lot of money, so I wanted to celebrate. That's why I got the presents."

"And what do you have to do?" Billy was looking up to Joe with huge eyes. Joe ignored the awe in his innocent face. Everything seemed to be going well and yet he hadn't even started. He took a deep breath.

"All I have to do is tell them where I found the rock. So remember, it's our secret. Don't tell anyone where I've been traveling lately."

"How are they going to know what the rock is like?" Billy asked softly.

Joe's heart sank. Billy's sharp mind had beaten him to it.

"I'll have to take it to them," Joe whispered.

"Not you," Billy said. "Mister Scherr will. That's part of the deal, right?"

"Yes."

"So Cory gets my crystal again."

He had figured it out. Joe spoke faster, just trying to be done quickly.

"Cory won't see it. Ever. His father is going to take it to a bunch of sales and marketing people. Lots of people are going to see what they think of it. If they like it, I might be able to make a lot of money. If not, then nothing is lost."

"So, will I get my crystal back?" Billy's thin, pale fingers curled protectively around the talisman hanging from his neck.

Joe sighed. "Of course, buddy. To be safe, that's why I got you all these presents, so you'll have plenty of gifts."

Billy looked away from him and shook his head. Joe started to say he was sorry, but the boy spun around, tears streaking down his face. "You're as bad as Cory the Asshole! You're taking my crystal. It's mine! You're an asshole, too!"

Teri smacked him. "Enough! You behave. Show respect. Joe brought these presents for you."

"Mom, he's stealing it like Cory did."

"Come on, Ace," Joe began, but Billy interrupted him.

"Keep it." Billy tore the crystal from his neck, fraying the twine necklace. He hurled it against the wall. It bounced high, scattering color around the room.

"Billy!" Teri screamed.

Her son stomped up the stairs to his room and slammed the door, leaving Teri and Joe among a pile of crumpled wrapping paper.

2

"Welcome to the Spy Room."

The marketing manager chuckled. Ethan Scherr spat out a fake laugh. Joe grunted, but didn't comment. He had met so many people at MajorCo Toys Corporation's New Product Division in the last hour, he couldn't remember any names. He simply followed behind Scherr and the herd of marketing specialists.

They marched through the cold, marble gray floors, crushing into a small, dark room. A giant window of one-way glass was set into the room's far wall. It reminded Joe of the countless TV police dramas, when the officers observed an interrogation. The difference here was that instead of a single table with two chairs in a drab room, beyond this glass was a child's playroom paradise.

Toys, crafts, and crayons were everywhere in brightly colored cubbyholes and strewn among the plastic furniture, all products of MajorCo Toys. Children of varying ages played and interacted with two adult caretakers. Each child was wearing a different-colored shirt with a number on it.

"The numbers are their ages. None are over nine. We use our employees' children for marketing research, and the parents get free daycare. It's win-win for everybody," one of the executives said. The bright colors made Joe squint.

The marketing manager stepped to the side and indicated a speaker box set into the wall. "The nannies are equipped with earpieces. We can talk to them through this terminal." He pressed the button and spoke. "Eileen, can you bring out the newest toy? Thank you, dear." He released the button and stepped back.

"You won't believe these results," he said, standing between Joe and Ethan, clapping each on the shoulder. "It's just like you said, Scherr, kids want this thing so bad, they'll beat up other kids with cancer for it."

Joe looked sideways at Scherr who smiled weakly and shrugged, then turned his attention to the one-way glass.

Eileen the nanny looked to the one-way glass and gave a subtle nod. She tucked her short blond hair behind her ear and rose from the circle of children, making sure each was occupied with their art projects. The other nanny watched Eileen and threw her hands up and cheered as a well-timed distraction.

With the speed of a magician, Eileen slipped her hand behind a cabinet, and pulled out the crystal Joe had brought back from Palagua. Eileen stepped across to an empty craft table and set the crystal there slyly, a rainbow rocking on the ceiling as it balanced.

The two nannies announced, "Free time, everyone," and disconnected themselves from the circle of children. They moved to their desks, pretending to do paperwork.

The children were involved with their toys and projects, staring down at them. "As soon as one of them notices it, we'll…"

"Start time!" one of the marketing team called out. A two-year-old had noticed the crystal. He immediately dropped his plastic truck and staggered on uneasy child legs towards the table. "Five seconds," the time-keeper said. The team mumbled with excitement.

Joe looked at Scherr, who winked at him.

"Ten, eleven, twelve, thirteen, fourteen," the time-keeper called out, louder as the child came closer to the crystal, colorful bars widening on her face. "Time!" someone called at seventeen. One of the team made notes on her clipboard. The room cheered silently, then loudly shushed itself.

"Seventeen from introduction to discovery. Count time from discovery to desire." The time-keeper counted up again.

The two-year was holding the crystal, turning it in his hand, utterly fascinated.

"This is awesome," someone said, slapping Joe on the back.

From across the playroom, a tall five-year-old chewing his thumb took notice. After a few seconds, he stomped toward the two-year old. He snatched the crystal and walked away. The two-year old began crying.

"Fantastic!" the marketing department manager said. His team gurgled their approval. "It never fails. Less than a minute from introduction to discovery to desire. Best numbers we've ever had."

Scherr joined in the celebration and high-fives. "Market penetration in under sixty seconds, baby!"

The rest of the children followed the five year-old, chasing the crystal. He held it behind his back, but a shorter, stockier child kept reaching for it. Finally, the short kid punched the taller five-year-old in the nose. Blood poured down the crying child's face. The nannies leapt from their desks as the lone seven-year-old dived into the fray.

Children's limbs grappled over the fistful of color.

"Awesome!" The marketing team roared their approval, as the kicking, punching and crying intensified. "My money's on the ugly kid! Whose boy is that? Martha's?" The nannies glanced uneasily toward the one-way glass as they shouted for order.

The marketing manager turned to Joe and Ethan. "That's the best reaction we've ever seen. Usually the progression from introduction to discovery to desire is measured in minutes. By comparison, this is an instant. We want kids to be nuts for our toys and fast about getting there. Let me tell you, these focus groups don't lie. It's just like you promised, Scherr. Good job. This, gentlemen," he indicated the bloody, screaming, crying brawl beyond the one-way glass, "this is very good news."

3

The MajorCo Toys company logo hung high on the wall, a silver icon overlooking the large boardroom and the huge table that filled it. Each of the twelve seats was occupied with representatives from MajorCo Toys' New Product Division. Joe and Ethan sat at one end, facing the expectant executives. The tiny piece of crystal rested in the middle of the table, casting a feeble rainbow into the void of marble, metal and polished wood.

"I'm happy with this," Ethan said, thumbing through the dozen-paged contract.

His lawyer nodded. "My client speaks for both of us."

Everyone turned to Joe. "So what do you think?" The CEO of MajorCo Toys asked him.

Joe took a deep breath.

"I think what I've thought from the beginning. What I mentioned from the start. I'm concerned about the native people. This is their land. Do we have a promise that, once I give the exact location, we will get an agreement from them?"

The CEO answered him. "We will discuss the matter with all the proper government authorities. Everything will be legal regarding the United States, and whatever this other nation is."

Joe replied, choosing his words carefully. "While I do care about the nation, I want to make it clear that I am referring to the native people. The ones who live on this land. Will you wait for their okay?"

"They usually aren't part of international trade agreements. That would complicate things immensely."

The room was quiet and Joe knew his answer. "Until then, we don't have a deal."

"At least, tell us the country you're referring to," the CEO persisted. "At least do that. Then perhaps we can begin to work on the government piece of our pending agreements."

Joe turned to his lawyer, Sheldon, who nodded.

"As a sign of good faith," the CEO said.

"What if I tell you the country and then you find out where the crystal is on your own?"

The CEO folded his hands and from across the room spoke as if he were addressing a child. "There has to be a little give and take. You have the disclosure agreement we signed when you first approached us. If we sneak to wherever it is and start production, you can sue us. Okay? But I assure you that screwing you is not in our best interest. Our lawyers would cost more than whatever you would win. Now, please. Sheldon, help us out here?"

Joe looked at his lawyer again. "It's okay," Sheldon said. "Just the country. A sign of good faith."

Joe looked around the room at the expectant faces. "All right," he mumbled. "Palagua."

"Where the hell's that?" one of the marketing team blurted. The CEO glared at him until he slumped in his seat.

* * *

At lunch, Joe, Scherr and their lawyers ate together. The lawyers were silent, but Scherr's cheeks were bright red. He was obviously furious.

"Joe, what the hell are you thinking?" he barked, "We're on the doorstep!"

Joe forced a calm reply. "I'm just trying to do right by the native people. That's all. If we get that taken care of, that's good enough."

"If you put up too much resistance, then you'll get nothing."

"I already told them the country, and we're all committed to a deal. This is just a detail I need ironed out."

"They'll find a way around it if you don't give in soon."

"What about the contract? What the boss said? I could sue. I'll do it if I have to."

"Please," Scherr said. "You're holding us all back from making money. You play tough out too long, they'll find a way to just cut you out. Stop this crap, man!"

Neither man said a word for the rest of their lunch.

4

The following day, negotiations resumed. The executives gathered around the table. Joe noticed few of them made eye contact with him.

"We have a special guest with us today," the MajorCo Toys CEO announced. A short, well-dressed, dark-skinned man was ushered into the boardroom. He nodded and walked right to Joe, clasped his hand and shook firmly.

"A pleasure to meet you, my friend," the man said with a Latino accent.

"Joseph Vera," the CEO announced, "meet Manuel Carlos Galeno, ambassador from the great nation of Palagua to the United States."

Joe smiled. "You got the ambassador? Is this for real?"

"Palagua is always attentive to our business partners," Galeno said.

"Well, thank you for coming," Joe said.

The entire room sat down, Galeno choosing the seat directly next to Joe.

"So," Ambassador Galeno began, "I hear you enjoyed your stay in our beautiful country."

"I did."

"And you have found one of our many natural resources that our friends in the United States wish to work with us in harvesting."

"I did. But." Joe had trouble continuing. Manuel's eyes were so honest, his tone so measured, he felt like he was being hypnotized. Joe turned to his lawyer.

"Sheldon?"

Mora immediately jumped in, addressing the Palaguan ambassador. "My client has only one condition. The people who are living on this land must be taken care of and not harmed in any way. This will all be done pending their permission. Or not at all."

Manuel smiled, lighting up the room. "Of course, my friend," he said, touching Joe's hand. "Of course. There are hundreds of native peoples in our beautiful nation. We are a fair government. We would be insulted if anyone thought or implied any different."

5

"So," Teri asked as Joe let himself into her house, carrying Chinese food take-out, "how's it going? How's the deal working?"

Joe sighed. "It's a pain. Lawyers and mumbo-jumbo. I want to make sure we proceed properly or not at all, but I feel like it's getting away from me. I can't talk about it now. I need a break. Where's the kid?"

"Upstairs. Sleeping. He's not feeling well. We went to the doctor's today." She turned away, breathing deeply. "Not so good."

"Hey," Joe said, rushing to her. "Hey. Come here." He hugged her as tears ran down her face. "You all right? What did they say? Be honest. You don't have to be tough around me."

She politely twisted away from his touch. "Nothing new. It's just not getting better, the cancer is holding its ground, so they increased his medicine, before we try the full-blown chemo. That's why he's sacked out."

"Come on," he said, leading her to the couch. "Just talk to me."

"I don't think he's going to be cured. Ever." She blew her nose. "I just don't."

"You don't know that."

"I know that's how I should feel, but... call it mother's intuition. I hope and I hope, but it's not enough. And I save money and I've got credit cards maxed out and my insurance is as high as it will go. And I don't think it's going to help. I feel like I'm betraying him by not believing. It's just a lot to deal with." She rested her head on his shoulder.

Joe stared at the wall, feeling the weight of her head and her hopes resting on him. She was silent for a long time. He didn't pressure her to talk. He guided her to the couch where she lay down and dozed off. He covered her with a blanket.

"Sometimes it's a lot," she mumbled in her sleep.

Joe crept to Billy's bedroom. He stared for a long time at the frail boy, his thin body barely making an impression under the sheets.

"Hang on, Ace," he whispered. "The cavalry's on the way."

* * *

Joe arrived at his lawyer's office early the next morning. They were meeting up before heading to another day of dealing with MajorCo's team.

"Good news, my friend," Sheldon said as he arrived.

"What's that?"

"Our buddy Manuel, the Palaguan ambassador, has come up with a plan for you. Whoever the native people are, he'll make an agreement with them. Nothing happens without them, and they will receive some of the profits from the mining operation. In his words, the land should pay for its own protection. These natives, whoever they are, will be able to ensure they own their own land."

"Good. Good," Joe said. "I'm tired of holding out. As long as you feel we've got something to protect the people living there, let's go sign this contract and make some money."

Sheldon laughed. "I like the way you think."

6

"Stop!" Ndiko yelled in Huapi as he raced along the mountain path.

"Stop!"

Three men were emerging from the sacred cave, picks and shovels over their shoulders, satchels full. Ndiko could tell by their pale skin they were Palaguans. They didn't understand his command, or they didn't care. As soon as they heard him yelling, two ran off. The last one approached, jabbing his shovel before him.

"What are you doing?" Ndiko screamed. The Palaguan stared at him, eyes darting in fear.

Ndiko pointed at the cave and yelled, "That is a gift to us! To my people from the gods! You shouldn't be in there!"

The man awkwardly swung the shovel like a club.

Ndiko caught the shaft beyond the blade and yanked it easily from the smaller man's grip. He spun the shovel and landed a blow to the Palaguan's side, crushing his victim's elbow, knocking him down. Pieces of crystal tumbled from the man's leather pouch.

"No!" Ndiko shouted. "The gods gave us those! The gods!" He stood over the man, shovel blade pressing into his twitching neck. "You fool!"

Ndiko's fear overpowered his rage, so he dropped the shovel and bent to his knees, desperately picking up the crystal shards as the Palaguan scrambled to his feet and staggered into the jungle, holding his shattered elbow. Ndiko looked up into the brush, wondering if he had recovered all that they stole.

"You fools!" he bellowed. He cradled the shards in his arm and raced inside the cave.

When he arrived at the central chamber, where the crystal lined the walls, he was exhausted, panting, sobbing.

"Most powerful gods, I am sorry," he said. "So sorry." He pressed the pieces into the gashes from where they had been pried. When he let go the stones fell loose. He licked the gash and pressed the shard in again. It held for only a second and slid away.

"Please," he cried, his breathing panicked. "Take it back!"

He pushed the pieces against the mother-rock and pressed for several minutes, until the blood ran from his hand and his arm was stiff.

He let go and the rock slid free. He picked it up and banged it on the cave floor several times, crying.

"Where did this come from?" he wailed.

He paced the cave, unable to calm down.

"Please forgive my father," he shouted, his cry echoing. "I'm trying to make it right."

One last time he attempted to repair the damage, but the rock didn't stay. He left the pieces in a small pile, each one carefully set near from where it was wrenched loose.

Part 5

1

Teri adjusted her pajama top and sweatpants as she ran down the steps. Someone was knocking, not with urgency, but persistent. She peeked outside and yanked open the door.

"What the hell, Joe?"

He smiled at her, a drunk smile, but lacking the stench of booze.

"It's late," he said. "I mean early. I think. I'm sorry. I just had to talk to someone."

"Why? What's wrong? I haven't heard from you in a couple days."

He stepped in. "I just had to absorb the news. I've been up since... I can't remember when. Two, three days."

"News? What news? Good? Bad?"

"Good. Very good."

"You haven't been drinking, have you?" she giggled nervously.

"No. But I feel like it."

"That girl you met in Palagua, she's not... pregnant?"

Joe looked at her confused. "Nina? I haven't spoken to her since that night," he said. "I don't think she's pregnant. Who said we ever-"

"Oh, it's you," Billy said without enthusiasm from the top of the steps. He reluctantly came down, rubbing his eyes. "What's up?"

"Was it your meeting? With MajorCo Toys?" Teri asked.

"Hello, Billy," Joe said. "Yes. The meeting went very well." He laughed and looked away, adding, "I just feel weird."

"Weird? Do you want some coffee? Weird how?"

"Sure. Coffee would be good. I'll make it. You just woke up."

"So, will you tell me what the hell this is about?"

Billy followed them into the kitchen.

"We signed a contract," Joe said. "They anticipate this being big. Huge. They gave me a signing bonus. Just to tell them where it was. Specific details on where I had been in Palagua. That was it."

"That's great."

"I quit my job," he laughed. "It was as fun as I had imagined. I went right up to the people I didn't like and told them what I thought. They were powerless, but it got old fast. So I left."

"You quit. But then…" Teri looked at him.

"That's right," he said.

"That advance signing bonus must have been pretty big."

He nodded, smiling stupidly.

"How much?"

He whispered in her ear.

Teri dropped her coffee mug into the sink. "Oh, my God."

"You're rich?" Billy asked.

"Hell yeah!" he yelped, pounding the counter. Then, much quieter, he added, "And that's just the beginning, before my percentage of sales. I'm afraid to say it, like I might jinx it, like I might wake up."

Teri collected her broken coffee mug. "No school for you, mister," she pointed to Billy. "We're going to celebrate."

"Damn right," Joe said.

Billy fought back a grin, watching his mother and Joe dance around the kitchen.

"Do I get my crystal back?"

"Oh, honey," his mother said, "Joe will buy you a thousand other things. Be happy now. Come on."

Billy joined in reluctantly, but only after he mumbled aloud, "I still want it back."

2

Ndiko's father and mother were following him closely as they pushed through the small entrance to the cave. Ndiko turned his head and spoke to them over his shoulder.

"I didn't want to bring everyone to see this for fear of dishonoring you, father."

They emerged into the cavern, rainbows dancing over them, awash in the colorful light of the gift from the gods.

"Here."

Ndiko pointed to a portion of the crystal that hugged the cave wall at waist-height. Grey jagged scratches scabbed over the surface, muting the colors beneath.

Maubombo ran his fingers over the scars. He stared at them, then rose, silent.

"You see?" Ndiko said. "The pale men have come. And they take our gift."

His father turned away.

Yuala ran her fingers over the scars as well, quickly bringing her other hand to her mouth. A gasp escaped.

"You see?" Ndiko asked her.

"There are other things," Maubombo said.

"Other things?" Ndiko said. "What are you talking about?"

"There are other things our tribe should worry about."

"But this is a gift from the gods. And you let the pales take it. You gave it to him."

Maubombo spun and jabbed a shaking finger in his son's face.

"The pale man takes what he wants. This mere rock is not the foundation of our village. The gods have given us gifts far greater than this."

"Mere rock? Other gifts? You don't care. Mother, do you hear him?" He spat on cave's floor. "He doesn't even care."

Maubombo shot back, "I gave it as a gift to one of the few pales who deserved it. We must establish bridges with them, or they will continue to erode our numbers and our land until there is nothing left."

"Ndiko," Yuala said softly, "why must every day be like this? Why can't you be more like your friend, Waho? He has a family, he has the most kind and respectful nature. Why must you always be so angry? What did your father and I do to you?"

Ndiko snorted. "Waho is my friend and always will be. But he's not going to be chief. He doesn't make decisions. He lets his wife tell him what to do."

"So do I," Maubombo chuckled. "It's the only way to get a wife."

Yuala glared at him. "Now is not the time for joking."

Ndiko snorted, pointing to the stabbed crystal. "Exactly. How can you make jokes? After this?"

"I told you, son," Maubombo said, "we must learn to live with the pales."

Ndiko spat. "This is your plan, then? Survival by appeasement? By giving out our last secret?"

Maubombo hung his head, turned, and walked back toward the village without a word. His face was stern, revealing no emotion.

"Father! Father! Come back. Coward! Idiot! Mother, do you see?"

"Yes! I see!" she cried. "Now stop. Just stop this! He did what he did. Let it go."

"It is no longer my choice."

"You have so much anger," she said, "I don't understand. In this beautiful place."

"I am angry, but I did not bring it here." He looked after his father. "I know where it came from."

3

Teri and Joe waved and screamed each time the carnival ride swung Billy past them. He lifted both hands off the safety railing.

"Be careful!" Teri yelled.

Joe laughed.

"He's so happy," she said, smiling.

"I'm glad. You're both doing well with the rules I laid out. No 'Can I?' and no 'Are you sure?' It's like you two are naturally rich."

"I can get used to this, riding in a limo, buying whatever I want. I'm not going to complain. Today's been the most fun I've had in a long time. If we're the natural leeches, you're the natural benefactor. The born bachelor playboy."

Billy spun by again, screaming. They waved.

"I'm not all fun and games," Joe said, "I can get him treatment. The best available. The best money can buy."

"I know you can."

"Well, I'm going to. Like you said, I'm a bachelor. I don't need the money."

"Thank you," she said, waving again.

"He's going to get the finest treatment anyone can get."

Teri looked at him and smiled. "I don't think that's going to help."

"What? Are you kidding? Why so negative? Doctors can do a lot. Especially when you give them money."

"Sure, they can keep the body alive, but…" she trailed off.

"We're going to do the best we can. Don't be such a pessimist."

"I'm just a realist. Money can do a lot, but not everything." She smiled weakly. "Is all that cash going that deep into your head already?"

"Don't be ridiculous."

Teri waved at Billy as he spun by again. "Just don't change," she said, not looking at Joe. "I like you how you are."

4

"How much?" the American senator asked. "No way. Now come on, Marcos. Michelangelo. Whatever your name is. We both know any purchase of this size will be a huge boost to your economy. You can't export bananas forever."

"Manuel. My name is Manuel Carlos Galeno," the Palaguan ambassador said, "And our nation's pride will prevail. Besides, we have to negotiate with the native peoples on that land as your contract stipulates. It's a costly and delicate process."

The senator rolled his eyes and made no attempt to hide it. "Do you know how much money our corporate economy is willing to invest here? I could take it somewhere else."

The ambassador shook his head. "I am not stupid, senator. If you could, you would have. We wouldn't be talking at all."

The senator began to twitch.

"Well, Manny, as we Americans say, you drive a hard bargain."

"I drive a fair bargain. And I do not allow my land to be raped."

"Aw, hell. Well, that's why you're not a good businessman."

The senator laughed. The ambassador did not.

"That's a joke, son."

"No," Manuel corrected, "this is no joke. We are already looking into other potential buyers. As you say in America, am I making myself clear?"

He bowed slightly.

The senator frowned.

"Bring the price down, or we don't have a deal, and I'll have to apply pressure through the free trade agreements."

"The Palaguan government does not feel that the free trade agreements are fair to our country."

"So what? It's still the ruling document. Now bring the price down. You went through all that trouble with MajorCo Toys and now you're standing in the way."

"No. You are wasting my time. Clearly MajorCo wants this terribly. They must feel it will bring huge profits. Why else would they have brought in a mighty senator? Unless he's a stockholder and this is part of his self-interest."

The senator lowered his voice to a growl. "Don't play hard-ball with me, Manny. And I don't appreciate the false accusation. I'm trying to help you."

"The terms I have offered stands. Americans do not let anything get in the way of what they want. Your foreign policy has never said anything otherwise." Manuel finally allowed himself a smile.

"Don't you ever forget it," the senator said, rose and walked out.

5

"What's that noise?" someone called. The entire Huapi village was vibrating. Children stopped their playing and began to cry.

"Is the boat returning?" Yuala yelled, scooping up a child in each arm, comforting them.

"No," Ndiko said, "it's coming from the direction of the cave." He grabbed his spear.

"Come with me!" he called to the older boys. "Bring your weapons!"

"Son," Yuala said, standing in front of him. "Don't."

The babies in her arms wailed.

"I'll be all right, mother."

Maubombo emerged from his hut. "What's that noise? What's happening?"

"Quickly!" Ndiko said to the cluster of young men around him. They bolted into the woods, following their leader.

"Son, wait!" Maubombo called.

"I know what is happening," Ndiko said to the young men around him, "The pales are coming to steal the gift from the gods. They have brought their machines to tear apart our land."

He dashed trough the forest, his clan behind him. They headed toward the deafening rumble, its sound punctuated by a louder cracking. As they arrived at the source of the thunder, the jungle's canopy rained small animals and fruits. A terrible smell wafted through the air, burning their noses.

Half the young men turned and ran.

"Cowards!" Ndiko called after them. His friend Waho's lower lip trembled. Ndiko grasped his arm tightly.

"Be strong."

Waho nodded, but continued to shake.

Ndiko led them forward slowly, crouching as a great yellow-orange slab of metal grabbed a tree in its claw and tore it from the ground.

"Where did that come from?" one of the Huapi hissed.

"They are devils!" another cried.

Their eyes were wide with terror. Ndiko felt his hands become wet on his spear. The awesome might of the thing before him was frightening, but he stood his ground.

"Look in our water!"

One of the boys was pointing to the creek that flowed past their village. The normally clear water had turned a greasy brown.

"How will we drink?" someone cried.

"Silence. Be still. Be calm," Ndiko said, his solid voice calming the others. "See that thing? It is the pale man's spear. That is all. There is a man inside it."

Ndiko pointed to the cab of the machine, where a man operated the controls. Another tree was torn apart. The smaller ones were crushed. A truck and several men on foot, carrying tools, followed behind.

"Remember," Ndiko said, "it is but a spear. If you kill the man, the spear can hurt you no more."

The trust and awe in their eyes washed away Ndiko's own doubt. Another tree was uprooted and stuffed into the back of the machine with a roar.

"All of you go there," Ndiko pointed. "And yell, just make noise. That will distract them. I will kill the man."

The entire party, except for Ndiko, moved through the woods, in the opposite direction of the truck. Between the crashing noises, Ndiko whistled. The Huapi boys began shouting and cursing from their hiding place. The machines kept moving forward, but the Palaguan men withdrew behind the lead machine, gathering on the other side of the foliage, near where the shouting was coming from. The front machine proceeded forward alone.

"My weapon versus yours," Ndiko said.

He stepped from the jungle and raised his spear. The driver of the machine released the controls, stopping the claw in mid-air. The glass front of the cab exploded inward. Ndiko's spear punched through the driver's chest and pinned him to the seat. The machine whined deeply, choked and was still. The driver clutched at the spear, trying to pull it out, but his hands slipped on his blood. He lost his strength and hung there, his head and arms slack.

The machines behind the leader stopped, halting the entire caravan.

The Huapi men cheered. "Ndiko! Our leader! Our hero! What bravery!"

Ndiko dove back into the woods before the white men could see him.

The Palaguans were shouting at each other, running in all directions.

"Hurl your spears!" Ndiko yelled. "Attack them!"

The Huapi launched a wave of spears into the crowd of panicked Palaguans, but only two found their mark, neither fatally. Then from behind the truck, Ndiko heard several popping sounds. The leaves around his friends danced. Blood blew out the backs of his boyhood friends as the Palaguans answered the attack with gunfire.

"Run! Run!" Ndiko yelled. "Back to the village!" He stumbled backwards, racing for home, horrified. The rest of the group that was able followed him. Three of his friends were left back near the machine. They were bleeding, dying, dead.

The surviving boys stumbled through the jungle back home, wailing, covered with blood. The Huapi village was plunged into chaos as men and women rushed to them.

Ndiko looked around. "Where's Waho?" he screamed. "Waho? Where are you? No. No. No." His heart pounded.

"Waho, my friend, where are you?"

He pushed through the yelling and crying, calling for his friend.

"Waho!"

Tears ran down his cheeks, as he turned each boy to face him, but still could not find his friend.

"Waho!" he screamed as loud as he could. His voice broke through the chaos around him.

"Ndiko!" a voice called back. Ndiko followed it. There was Waho, standing before him, tears running down his face, the blood of their peers flecked over his torso.

Ndiko hugged him. "Waho! I love you. I love you, my friend." They hugged as the crying of the village swirled around them.

Ndiko pushed himself free. "I must go back."

"Go back?" Waho cried. "Why?"

"To see if anyone is still alive."

"Ndiko. Don't."

Ndiko turned away.

Waho's scream was lost in the wailing around them.

"Come back!"

6

Nina was on her way to visit the Huapi, surprised to find that past the Christian mission where the jungle should have begun, was a gaping hole. A large truck rumbled through the opening, crushing the tree stumps continued onto the main road of the city, heading for the docks. Crowds of workers carrying tools were trudging down the new road into the jungle. A caravan of bulldozers was pushing through the green with a sickening crunching and crackling noise, heading toward Huapi land.

Nina started to follow when a Palaguan armed with a rifle stepped in front of her.

"No. No one goes here."

"What's happening?" she asked, smiling flirtatiously.

"Business. That's all you need to know. Now leave."

"All right," she said, walking back the way she had come. She followed the edge of the forest, back into Palagua City until she was out of sight of the new road's entrance. She cut through one of the many makeshift neighborhoods backed up against the always advancing vines, and entered the jungle there.

Moving along a wide arc, she crashed through the jungle until she was parallel with the lead bulldozer. Hacking through the persistent foliage was strenuous. She was covered in sweat and exhausted, but driven by concern.

"This is not good at all," she said, stopping to get her camera and water from her backpack.

All day, the line moved through the jungle, destroying as it went. Behind the lead bulldozer, workers loaded trucks with the remains of trees. The trucks then raced back down the newly made path to unload somewhere and return ready for more.

The day wore on slowly, the sun creating a humid fog under the jungle canopy. She moved as close as she dared to the workers' column, taking pictures of the machines and men. Though slow, they never stopped creeping forward, the trucks hauling out endless piles of green.

As the sun neared the horizon, she knew they must be close to Huapi land by now. The men began to thin out, the workday ending, but the lead machine kept going.

Suddenly, there were shouts, then gunshots from the front of the line. Nina crouched down and waited, her heart pounding. The lead machine stopped. The men were screaming and running in all directions. They boarded a truck that retreated down the road toward the city. Abandoned, the bulldozer stalled and stopped.

Where there had been constant noise now there was only the dusk and silence.

Nina slowly rose and headed into the cloud of gunpowder. An eerie quiet settled among the smog.

After making sure she was alone, she approached the front bulldozer. It was still. She circled it, and saw the spear sticking out of the cab, the driver slumped over.

"My God," she whispered. Shivers raced over her skin. She took a picture and kept moving, almost slipping on the slick mud flattened smooth by the machine.

The vehicle's huge array of four back tires was parked partially on the tiny creek that supplied the Huapi village its drinking water. The water rose up against the tires and rerouted, carrying mud, oil and grease down toward the settlement.

She circled to the other side of the machine, and found the bodies of three young Huapi boys. Her hands shook as she snapped the pictures. The camera slipped through her fingers, slick with tears and sweat. She no longer looked through the viewfinder; instead, she let the camera do the looking. She had to keep her eyes closed anyway, the flies were gathering around the corpses.

The Huapi boys lay sprawled in twisted, bloody heaps, behind foliage cut down to waist-height. A sound came from one of the twisted corpses, a mechanical exhaling. She jumped. A fly landed on the corner of one boy's unblinking eye.

She gave a silent, guilty thanks that none of the boys or the driver gave any indication they were still alive. There was no way she could have brought them to medical aid if they had been.

A point pushed into her back. She fell to her knees, raising her hands.

"What are you doing?" someone behind her said in Huapi.

Ndiko raised his spear and prepared to drive it through the pale woman. Feeling the point pull back, Nina turned, tears in her eyes. Ndiko held the spear, shaking. She raised her hands and held her palms toward him, trembling. He stepped toward her, aiming for her heart.

"One pale won't come close to avenging them," he said, "but it is something."

"I'm sorry," she said in Huapi.

Through the fog of his rage, he recognized her. She had been with the man who had saved his father's life. She spoke Huapi. Incredibly, she spoke it well. It was all too confusing. His spear-tip began to shake.

Nina spoke again, the flies and sorrow thick in her mouth, breaking her voice. "I have to do something. I want to help."

Ndiko lowered his spear and stared at the corpses for a long time. Nina's knees started to ache. She didn't dare move. The crazed anger in his bulging eyes terrified her.

Finally, Ndiko pointed to her camera. "Is that what will help? The box that flashes? Why does every white person have one? What does it do?"

"This," she said, "is the eye of the pale world."

"Even if they could see me, they couldn't understand what I say," he set down his spear and sat on the earth, staring between his legs.

"Some will understand," she said, "some like me. And they will want to help you. They will be saddened by this."

Ndiko wasn't listening. He shuddered and wailed over the dead bodies, "There is no help you can offer. My friends, my friends."

Nina wrapped her arms around him and he buried his face into her breasts, crying like a child.

"Ndiko," she said, soothingly, holding his face in her hands and looking into his eyes.

"I promise I will do something."

7

"Right here, Mom!" Billy chirped from the passenger seat.

"Are you sure?" Teri said, lifting her foot off the car's accelerator. She leaned over to look through the windshield at the large home before them. "It's huge."

"That's what his directions say."

"Oh, my God."

She pulled her minivan into the semi-circular gravel driveway, stopping behind two luxury cars already parked. She and her son stared up the steps that led between two white columns to the front door.

"Holy crap," Billy said.

"That's what I was thinking," Teri said.

They exited the car and walked up the steps to the entrance.

"Everything is white," Billy noted, touching the fake marble columns and the door frame. They could hear voices inside.

"Hello?" Teri called as they pushed the door open, revealing a large open living room receiving area. A staircase spiraled in the background, leading to the second floor. Joe Vera and Ethan Scherr were talking excitedly in the middle of the empty room.

"Welcome," Joe said, smiling broadly, holding out his arms. "Welcome to my new home!"

Billy ran toward him and hugged him. Joe smiled and rubbed the boy's head while looking up at Teri. She was grinning, scanning the vast space.

"Everything is so clean," she said, "so new."

"It's got that new house smell, doesn't it?" Scherr said, breathing deeply. Teri smiled close-lipped and looked away from him.

"Let me give you the tour," Joe said, prying himself loose from Billy's hug.

"Joe, this is like a castle!" Billy yelled, running across the room.

"He's a rich man now," Scherr said to Billy. "And he's just getting started. You'll be amazed the things that money brings to you." He grinned broadly at Teri. She shivered and looked away again.

"All right. I've got to be going," Scherr said. "Congratulations on the new home, Joe. I'll see you at the office tomorrow. Nice to see you again, Billy. Teri."

He let himself out.

Billy started up the steps, counting them.

"That guy is slimy," Teri said. "I don't like him."

Joe chuckled. "He's a little shifty, but he made the deal go through. I thought he was full of crap." He swept his arm to indicate his new home. "Looks like he wasn't."

Billy topped the spiral steps and vanished down the hall.

"Billy!" Teri called.

"No. Wait," Joe said. "Let him go. Let him explore for a while. We need to talk. We need to plan on getting him in a new cancer treatment program. My money isn't just about this home. It's about him, too."

"That's going to be hard to get used to."

Joe smiled. "I guess we'll have to work through it together."

8

Nina sat in the United States embassy, fanning herself with her papers and photos. It had taken her nearly all day to get here. Even though she was a resident of Palagua City and the embassy was based there as well, moving among the masses of people was never a quick task.

The buses were so packed she had to wait for three to leave without her. There were crowds everywhere, and then a traffic jam had stopped them up for hours. Palagua City was a sprawling metropolis in a small nation. Nina could appreciate the often-mentioned phrase, "Palagua City is Palagua."

"Ms. Vasquez, the assistant will see you now," a friendly woman behind a desk said.

"The assistant? I want to see the ambassador."

"He's very busy. Everyone can't just go right to the top."

"All right."

An elderly man emerged from the offices behind the front desk. He was dressed in a button-down shirt, a tie, and shorts. He wore his long white hair in a ponytail. They shook hands.

"Ms. Vasquez?"

"Yes. Call me Nina."

"I'm one of the ambassador's assistants. Thomas Donnelly."

He led her to a secluded table on the deck of the embassy building. They sat under an umbrella, talking for over an hour. She told him the whole story of the three Huapi murders and the death of the worker.

"Oh, my God," he said, looking at her photographs. "Terrible. This is awful."

"Is there anything we can do?"

"Did you go to the police?" Donnelly asked.

"I don't entirely trust them."

"Smart move."

"I thought you could lend weight to the complaint."

"Of course. I will bring this up with the Ambassador next chance I get. I can't promise anything, but I'll try."

* * *

After an exhausting trek home, partially riding the bus and partially walking (one of the bus routes wasn't functioning) Nina collapsed on her bed, just in time for her phone to ring.

"Ms. Vasquez?"

The voice on the phone sounded familiar, but the signal was fuzzy. "Yes?"

"It's Tom Donnelly. I spoke to you earlier today, from the embassy."

She was genuinely surprised to hear from him so soon. "I remember."

"I, um, I'm sorry to tell you this, but basically the Ambassador laughed me out of his office."

"He did? Why?"

"I quote, 'We've got threats of a revolution, and that land holds the biggest potential money-maker Palagua has ever seen. We can't worry about some natives causing trouble for a mining team.' End quote."

Nina pressed her palm into her forehead. "That's not good."

"No. I'm sorry. Of course I feel bad for the Huapi, but... well, you know reality."

"I do."

"He did seem somewhat aware of the situation. Apparently the deaths at the mine have slowed things. They're having trouble recruiting workers. They're losing them to rumors about the Huapi, and possibly to the Palaguan Revolutionary Movement. The investors in the mine are tense. You've got big money on one side and the Huapi on the other. If sides have to be drawn, I think you know where the ambassador will line up."

"I understand."

"Sorry I couldn't be more help."

"Thanks for trying."

She hung up the phone and lay back on her bed, rubbing her temples in slow circles.

Part 6

1

"Hooray! Hooray! Hooray for Crystal Clay!"

An ethnically diverse gathering of children danced around in a colorful half-real, half-cartoon land, showing off the different shapes of their crystals.

"Twelve different shapes for you to enjoy! Collect them all!" a cheerful woman's voiceover encouraged. The children marched over a rainbow made by the crystal's rays and enhanced by computer graphics. Colors twisted and bent, all at the whim of the children. They smiled as the rainbow whipped them into outer space for a game of catch (using their crystals) with some passing aliens.

"There's color in every day. With Crystal Clay! Crystal Clay is a registered trademark of MajorCo toys."

The video ad ended. Everyone blinked as the lights in the boardroom flickered on.

"Good stuff," Ethan Scherr said.

Joe nodded, "Looks great to me. But, I still don't like 'clay.' You can't reshape it."

The room was silent for a beat. Scherr answered. "But it rolls off the tongue. Marketing isn't always about logic, it's about feeling." Nods percolated around the room. Joe frowned.

"Well," Scherr continued, "I'm glad you all like the ad."

Then began a lengthy, jargon-filled discussion of their pre-Christmas marketing strategies. Joe immediately shut the discussion out and allowed himself to daydream about what he could spend his money on next.

That night, Joe played the message on his answering machine.

"Hi, Joe, this is Nina. Remember me? From Palagua? Please call me. It's very important. Extremely important. Some Huapi have been killed and at least one Palaguan miner. Please call. Thanks."

He stared at the "delete message" button and flopped backwards on his bed, phrases clashing in his mind.

He heard Teri crying about Billy, "Sometimes it's a lot." He heard Nina's message saying "Extremely important."

He stared at the ceiling until sleep took him.

2

Nina called Joe again but hung up without leaving a message when he didn't answer. She decided to care for some errands since her pantry was almost empty. Exiting the grocery store, she passed two young men handing out small red slips of paper.

"Would you like to make a better life for Palagua?" one of the boys asked her.

Nina shifted her bag of goods to her left arm and took the flyer.

"Join the PRM, the Palaguan Revolutionary Movement!" it read. "Build a better life for all Palaguans. Help Palagua become a stronger nation."

"I'll think about it," she said, taking the paper and walking away quickly. It was a difficult situation. If she threw the paper away, they were more likely to harass her. If she took it and a government agent saw her, he might throw her in jail. She watched as the other shoppers exiting the market had the same debate play across their face.

Palagua was a beautiful place, but for some reason the price of natural beauty often seemed to be living among social tension.

She was impressed with the pamphleteers' boldness. Recruiting for the PRM in some places was met with violence by the police.

The pamphleteer near her moved on to help his partner, who was discussing the PRM with two teens.

"Palagua doesn't have much to offer," the recruiters said. "It's either this or work in the mine on the edge of the city."

Nina set down her brown bag, eavesdropping.

"I heard some guy got killed at that mine," one of the boys passing by said.

"You're right. By the forest-people. The Huapi."

"Yeah, they ate his whole body."

"I heard they cut off his ears."

"Did they?"

"My uncle's friend was one of the workers. He said the savages poured out of the forest, and killed a guy. The security guards fired into the forest, but then everyone took off. No one wants to go back for any amount of money."

"I need work, but I'm not taking a job like that."

"Me neither."

"Nobody is. They can't get the mine working right. Stupid government. They won't pay the workers extra risk pay, and now they're having trouble getting organized. You can bet the bosses aren't missing any money."

"The army should just kill those savages."

"The government should do a lot," the PRM recruiter said, "But it doesn't. That's why we want to change it. Wouldn't you rather you had more choices than just a job as a farm laborer where you die from a broken back, or a miner, where the Huapi kill you? Want more choices? Join the PRM!"

Nina hefted her bag and strode toward the conversation, her cheeks burning red, determined to interrupt.

"You've got it all wrong about the Huapi," she said. All four boys looked to her.

"Get out of here!" someone yelled before she could say more. The grocery store owner was waving a large steak knife. "Get out! You think you're revolutionaries? You stand for the working man?

Then don't bring the police to my store! They'll think it's a recruiting station!"

"Take it easy, old man. Don't you want a better Palagua?"

"I'll get a better Palagua when everyone stops trying to control it. Now get out."

The boys stepped back and kept talking. Nina took off. They were all raising their voices. A crowd was forming, as the owner lunged randomly. A police car screamed around a corner, sirens blaring, and nearly hit her. She quickened her pace home and didn't look back.

3

"So what do you think, Ace?" Joe asked.

"It's not bad," Billy replied.

"Not bad?" Teri said, indignant. "It's perfect."

The nurse guiding them through the pediatric cancer facility laughed. "Billy, I'm sure you'll learn to like it."

She turned to Teri and Joe. "We have plenty of staff and activities to keep him busy. We'll also help him adjust after receiving treatment. The counselors are here to help him, and you, deal with every aspect of this experience. He'll be surrounded by children just like himself, and you'll be surrounded by concerned adults like you."

"It's wonderful," Teri said. "And the counselor to patient ratio is?"

"We don't really speak in those terms. We have an entire team dedicated to each patient and his family. We also have teachers on hand to continue their education. The school environment makes daily life as mainstream as possible for the children."

"A whole team," Teri chuckled. "That's wonderful. That's... much more than the local hospital."

"Hospitals do the best they can. Since we are funded by each patient's family, we do the absolute best. We know the families have difficulties, and we can attend to them."

"But the cost," Teri began, looking at Joe.

"Is not a concern," he said.

The nurse smiled, pointing across the room. "I think your decision is made."

Billy was sitting on a couch, playing a video game with another patient. The other boy was bald, white as a sheet, so pale he was nearly translucent. He seemed to have no muscle mass at all, just a skeleton wrapped in skin. Billy looked like an athlete sitting next to him.

"I think so," Teri said. She threw her arm around Joe and kissed him on the cheek.

The nurse smiled. "Come with me and we can get the paperwork started."

They walked away. Teri kept looking back to where Billy and his new friend were playing.

4

"Where is my son? Where is he?" a weeping mother cried, "Where? Where did you take him? Why doesn't he return?"

She slapped Ndiko. He didn't react.

The Huapi streamed from the village, running. They stampeded past him toward the scene of the slaughter as he trudged the opposite direction until he sat in the village, alone and numb.

Slowly they came staggering back, crying, carrying the bodies between them. No one looked at him except Yuala. She touched him, but he didn't respond. His father busied himself with the rituals necessary for proper disposal of the dead. He didn't even look towards his son once.

"It's the end of our people. The end has begun," one of the mothers wailed.

The sorrow and crying carried deep into the night.

* * *

Ndiko shook the painful memories from his head. He had lost track of days since he had killed the driver and the gunmen had killed his friends.

The village had been quiet, in a sleepy routine ever since. The women went out to gather fruit quickly, coming back with only a meager harvest. The men were equally afraid to venture out, and their hunting take was just as paltry. Even the few children of the village lacked energy. Everyone complained that the water tasted foul.

Ndiko woke up deep in the night and crept through the forest to the south side of the mountain, past the abandoned machinery, along the cliffs. He stood there, looking to the stars, considering jumping and ending his life.

He liked the idea for a long time.

Just as his conviction to end it all hardened, the sun rose, its first beam of light lancing his eyes.

"No," he said, squinting and looking away, "I have to fix this."

He sighed and headed back to the village.

5

The helicopter landed in a clearing ringed by young Palaguan men. The sun was blazing and most of the men were shirtless. All of them wore shorts and some of them wore sandals. The rest were barefoot. Each one held a wooden spear. Some stood at attention; the others were in various states of clowning around, twirling their spears like batons or using them to strike others on the rump.

Three men departed from the helicopter. The largest man was elderly, rotund. His face bulged red under his white hair and puddles formed under each armpit of his pale blue suit. A thin man walked next to him, a native Palaguan, the translator. The third man was dressed in full military camouflage, wearing a cap and mirrored sunglasses. He chewed tobacco emphatically.

"Americanos!" one of the young men yelled. He was identified as a leader by his black t-shirt and black beret. The young men locked their spines to attention out of sync and shushed each other.

"Give me a break," growled the man in fatigues.

The Palaguan wearing the black beret extended his hand and walked out to meet the large man.

The American refused to shake the Palaguan's hand.

"I don't have much time and I don't want to know your name. This is a simple situation," he said. "The Palaguan government is being rather unfair in their trade practices and we..." He dabbed his forehead with a handkerchief. "Aw, hell. I don't need to explain. It's too hot."

The leader in the black beret nodded as the thin man translated.

The American continued speaking as he swabbed his face. "Right. Now, in my country, we have a holiday called Christmas."

"Sí. Navidad," the black beret said.

"I guess you've heard the song, too. Anyway, my point is, I'm counting on you not to forget this favor. We want a more reasonable price prior to... Navidad. Am I clear?"

The man in the black beret listened to the translation and nodded enthusiastically before presenting the young men around them with a solemn, sweeping movement of his arm.

"You will have it sooner, senator," the translator said. "Our army is ready and your words are clear."

"This is an army?" the American grumbled. "Lord help us. Just tell him I said 'Glad to hear it,'" he said, nudging the translator.

The senator gave a signal to the helicopter. The storage bay door on the back crashed down. Eight soldiers pushed out two large crates. The young boys fidgeted.

The senator spoke to the man in the black beret.

"A gift from the American people. We fully support the Palaguan Revolutionary Movement and your fight for democracy."

In accented English, the man in the black beret said, "Navidad comes a little early for us." He smiled broadly.

"That's right, amigo." The senator abruptly turned back to the helicopter, clapping the man in fatigues on the back. "Keep in touch, Colonel."

"Will do, sir."

The translator and the senator boarded the helicopter, which took off immediately after the loading bay door was lifted, closed and secured. From high above, the senator looked down as the crates were opened.

Camouflage-patterned uniforms, guns, and rocket-propelled grenades spilled out. The weaponry was mobbed by the young boys, who were kept back only by the colonel repeatedly firing a pistol into the air. The senator tapped the pilot on the shoulder.

"Make it snappy before those savages kill us all."

6

Ethan Scherr and the MajorCo Toys marketing team continued their discussion for hours. They seemed to enjoy every second of it. For them it was a lively conversation, a thrilling experience.

For Joe it was horribly dull, full of jargon he didn't care to understand. His boredom caused his emotions to cycle between irritation and anger. The money was great, but these meetings were as tedious as the ones at his old job, and they took much longer. The team had given up politely asking for his input. Now they simply skipped over him as they brainstormed.

He didn't protest, he just daydreamed more.

"And it seems like we're having some troubles with the first shipment," one of the MajorCo execs said.

The gasps of horror around the table focused Joe's attention. He thought about Nina's message, the one he had deleted from his answering machine.

"The Palaguan government has given us their blessing, invited us in," one of the many suits asked. "Why should there be any delay? Doesn't the USA have a free trade agreement with Palagua?"

Another executive chimed in, "They better get that shipment steady. We've got all these ads going live really soon. The command coming down from on high is go, go, go."

"I heard there's been some trouble with the locals," someone far down the table said.

Everyone looked at Joe. He didn't know what to say.

"It's probably nothing major," Scherr quickly added. "I'm sure our subcontractors will have it straightened out in no time. They need jobs down there. Palagua isn't the most sophisticated place in the world." He led the condescending laughter, stealing a glance at Joe, who frowned but shrugged.

Scherr continued, "They can't export bananas forever." That got more laughs.

"No need to worry about it at all," the marketing manager said. "I met with our CEO. I told him about the results of our focus group test, and he said he's got a guarantee from some people in international business circles that we'll get what we want. Probably at a cheaper price than we expect, too. He said, 'The shipment of crystal clay is coming. One way or the other.' I don't know what that meant, but let me say, I'll bet heads somewhere are going to roll if we don't get what we want."

"And no," the manager added, "they won't be our heads."

The tension in the room dissipated. Scherr glanced sideways at Joe, who went back to daydreaming.

At noon, during a rare break in the meeting, Joe invited Scherr to lunch, just the two of them. Scherr was obviously sad to part with his several new hip marketing friends, but he accepted.

Joe jumped right into the conversation. "Why don't you count me out of these meetings? This marketing business isn't for me."

Ethan laughed. "I understand. I love this stuff. The planning, the brainstorming. Sales. The excitement of rolling out a new product. I'm all about it. This is a blast."

"Well, not for me. I'm sure you can manage alone. I'm wealthier than I've ever been. I'm not contributing and I hate this crap."

"Call your lawyer, see if you can work it out. If you don't want to be here, you shouldn't."

Joe called his attorney Sheldon Mora and received a call back immediately. He was stunned at how easy it was. Being a high-profile client of a high-profile lawyer was a luxury he could get used to.

"I'll take care of it," Sheldon said right before they hung up, and Joe believed him.

7

"So I quit," Joe said, finishing his story, sharing coffee with Teri while Billy played a hand-held video game. "I just couldn't stand all those business meetings. I'll still earn the money from my profit-sharing agreement; I just won't earn my salary anymore. But who cares? I don't get a charge out of that stuff like Scherr does."

"You've quit two jobs in a small amount of time," Teri laughed.

"Speaking of," he reached in his pocket and handed Teri a check. "Why don't you take a vacation, too."

Teri looked at the check and her jaw dropped. "Are you serious? That's a lot."

"It used to be a lot. Not anymore."

"But I'm not sure I can take time off. I might not have the days."

"That's OK. Just consider it a gift."

"Joe…"

"No. No protest. Nothing. Just accept it. Now, subject change. I think I'm heading back to Palagua."

Billy looked up. "Can we come with you? Please, Joe! Mom?"

"I don't think that would be a good idea," Teri said to her son. "You need to stay here and stay healthy, go to school."

"But Mom! Joe quit work. Twice! Can't I quit school?"

Teri ignored him and squinted at Joe. "Going to check on that girl, huh?"

"No. Well, just to visit. I've been thinking of going back for a while. She left me a message yesterday, the first time I've heard from her since I got back. She said it was important. So I think I'll just fly down there to check it out. But we're just friends. Nothing more."

Teri grinned, devilishly. "Let me get this straight. She calls, and instead of calling back, you fly down there to surprise her and talk. But you're just friends. Come on, Joe. I'm a woman. You can't tell me lies like that."

"I'm going to visit," Joe insisted. "I think I'll surprise her."

"You're going to surprise her? Mister Romantic Millionaire?"

"Please. You're both driving me nuts."

Billy pulled on Joe's shirt. "I want to go, too. Mom, come on! He's rich! He'll pay. Right, Joe? You can do anything. You're like Odysseus, constantly traveling, having adventures."

Joe rested his hand on Billy's frail shoulder. "I'm not as smart with mythology as you are. Was Odysseus a good guy? Anyway, I need to go back there and get you another piece of the crystal."

"Really?"

"Really. I promise."

"Swear?"

"I swear."

"Don't swear, Joe," Teri said. "You don't know you'll be able to do that."

"I'll try," Joe said. "I'll try really hard."

8

"Take them," Nina said, holding out a packet of tablets.

"What are they?" Ndiko asked.

"They make the water safer to drink," she said. "Try it."

He hesitated.

She anticipated his question. "They came from friends in the USA. There are many like me who want to help. Some of us pales are good."

Ndiko grunted, skeptical. He twisted a white water-purification pellet between his thumb and index finger while standing over the oily creek. Since he had killed the truck driver, the vehicle's tires had rested on the path of the Huapi drinking water, polluting it with grease and other fluids dripping from the dormant machine.

Ndiko looked down at the slowly running water and dropped the tablet in. The current swept it away. He dipped his hand in, and lapped some water.

"It still tastes odd."

Nina restrained a laugh as he picked out another pellet.

"You have to give it time," she said.

He placed the tablet in his mouth and bit down, then scooped some water into his mouth.

"No, don't eat it!" she yelled.

"I'm not stupid," he said, spitting.

He held another tablet in his teeth.

He formed a scoop with his hands and picked up some water. He spat the tablet into his hand-bowl. The pellet dissolved, turning the clear water milky white. He lapped it up, swished it around in his mouth while wearing a puzzled look.

He swallowed.

"It tastes different. A little better, but still not correct."

"It will be safer for your people. Not perfect, but it should help some, and cut down on the stomach pains."

"How do I know I can trust you and your friends in the USA?"

Nina thought for a moment before replying.

"I'm not sure what I can do to convince you my intentions are good. Would I be here if I meant you harm?"

He stared at her from the opposite side of the creek.

"Well would I?" she asked.

He didn't reply.

9

Ndiko was having trouble sleeping. He stared toward the packet of water-purification tablets sitting hidden in a corner of his hut, under his few possessions.

Worries bounced around his mind, haunting him. His stomach refused to settle, a result of the tainted drinking water.

A shadow moved in the moonlight. His father appeared over him, signaling him to follow. Ndiko was puzzled and annoyed, but glad for something to do.

They made their way toward the sacred cave in the dark. Maubombo crept around the still truck, as if he were afraid he might wake it. He kicked at the tire resting in their drinking-water creek. The machine didn't budge.

They continued on without a word. Subdued colors beckoned them into the cave.

Silently, they climbed together through the tunnels, son helping father along. They passed the colorful lights of the gift from the gods and moved through a small exit higher up the mountain, to a ledge overlooking Palagua City.

"I wanted to take you here for a private talk," Maubombo finally said, not looking toward his son, staring out across the electric haze of the city at night. "See all those lights below? When I was a boy, none of that was there. All this land was ours."

"So you've told me before. We owned it all, but then the pales came."

Maubombo growled. "Be patient. Let me finish."

Ndiko folded his arms and his father continued.

"Your grandfather took me here when none of this was below, only days before he died. He explained to me that above all, I had to keep the Huapi way of life alive. 'I promise I will not witness the end of our people,' I told him. The pales have always taken much, he warned. I knew that and told him so. I was your age then, determined to be great. Like you."

Maubombo's voice cracked. Ndiko stared at him intently. Secretly, Maubombo was frightened. His son's gaze was so intense it seemed he would fight him over a single misspoken word. Did I stare at my father like that? Maubombo wondered.

Before he could go on, Ndiko interrupted. "Father, we are skilled hunters. We can kill them."

"You're not hearing what I'm saying."

"I know exactly what you are saying. You want me to carry on your promise. You want me to swear that I will not witness the end of our people. I will not. I will teach them to fight, the women and children, too. I will defend our people to the death. I accept the challenge, as you did."

"No, you have completely misunderstood. Look at this valley below. The pales do not stop when they want something. They told our ancestors they didn't need the land. But need is not what drives them. When they decided they wanted it, they took it."

"I will die before that happens."

"If you die, our people are lost. This is just the beginning. They are coming for our gift from the gods. The pales can murder beyond any resistance you can assemble. You don't think they'll leave their precious machines here, do you?"

"They haven't come back yet."

"You scared them for a few days, but they will return, and with more powerful weapons. I have seen it before."

Ndiko growled, "You feel I will fail where you succeeded? That keeping our people alive is too great a task for me?"

Maubombo closed his eyes and sighed heavily. He never looked so old to his son. "It is too great a task for anyone. Our lives are different. The end is here. They will destroy our land and unless you act, the Huapi will be annihilated as well."

"What would you have me do?"

"Promise me you will not fight them. Because you cannot win. They will return soon. Do not fight them. Endure. Dodge. Hide. Move. And if you must, join them. Take everyone to the pale god."

"Take the village to the so-called mission? That would be equal to our destruction."

"We are still Huapi without this land."

"Ridiculous! Other than slaves, what can we be without land?"

"Soon you will be chief, and you must learn to make decisions based on something other than your pride! All things end. All things die. Even me."

Ndiko was silent, finally understanding. "This isn't just about your promise. Or our people," his son asked, blinking rapidly. "You think you're going to die soon. How do you know?"

Maubombo sighed deeply. "If I allow myself to live much longer, my promise to preserve our people will be broken." He grasped his son by both shoulders. "You are a proud man. And so am I. Do not make promises. They are a trap baited with honor. Do not do as I did. Do not serve pride. Serve the Huapi."

"You intend to leave me with this burden? You ask me to serve the Huapi by leading them from the land that sustains them? You are the one who has brought the end you fear. You have drawn the pales here by giving them the gift from the gods. You made such a promise much more difficult to keep!"

Maubombo hung his head. "I have some regrets. That's what I'm trying to save you from."

He seemed about to say more, but stopped.

Ndiko sprang forward and gripped his father's hand. "I make the same promise as you did. I will not witness the end of our people. I also promise I will not run out on them through death, like my father plans."

Maubombo smacked him. "You were ready to kill yourself when your three friends died! Much greater pain awaits you as a chief. Death is one of the easier things you must face."

Ndiko scoffed. "I will endure it all. I will be a great chief, and I will defend our land. I promise."

"Perhaps you can negotiate a deal with the pales, so that they may move the tribe to a reservation."

"If you feel such a compromise will save us, then why not keep your will to live? You sound like a coward."

Maubombo hung his head. "I am so very tired."

"Didn't you hear me?" Ndiko stood close to his father. "I promise I will banish them from this land."

"The pales have taken over the world," Maubombo said, a tear sneaking down his face. "You cannot stop them. Do not be so bold with your promises."

"Too late," Ndiko said, standing tall.

Maubombo knew his son wanted nothing more than for his father to congratulate him on his bravery, but the pride that ran through them both spoke first.

"You fool. I came here to save you from yourself, and you have made it worse by promising something that cannot be. Your judgment will now be clouded, options closed off because of your arrogance."

"You brought me here to accept a defeat you would rather die than face, and you call me a fool for refusing to face it myself."

Both men stared at each other.

Ndiko turned away first, heading back into the cave. He turned back to his father. "Your lack of faith in me will be proven wrong."

Maubombo stood alone on the ledge, staring at the haze over Palagua City.

Part 7

1

"So this is how the rich live." Joe smiled to himself, stretching his legs in his first class seat as his plane landed in Palagua City.

"The rich" were no longer a mysterious group of people beyond his life. He was one of them now. A surprise visit to a friend in a foreign country was no big deal any more.

Actually, he reminded himself, this was more than a leisure trip. This was a surprise inspection of sorts. Was there really a problem with the Huapi? He was counting on everything being fine.

He had held out before telling MajorCo Toys where he found the crystal. His lawyer had inserted a clause to respect the Huapi into the contract. Joe had read it himself and approved its wording. There shouldn't be anything wrong.

A taxi dropped Joe off in the bustling center of Palagua City. He dodged chickens, vendors and shoppers, bumping his way through the improvised market stalls made of wood and corrugated metal. He charged on through the heat, the crowd and smells (some flavorful, most rancid).

He headed toward the waterfront. Palagua was much as he remembered it: dusty, noisy chaos. One thing noticeably different were the Palaguan Revolutionary Movement's presence. On several corners, adding to the noise and crowds were the PRM faithful: mostly young men, teens even, standing on boxes, shouting into crackling bullhorns.

Police marched through the streets in large gangs, tearing down red banners, the young men dispersing before them.

He had seen a few of the rebels on his last visit, but they were obviously gathering support. It seemed their red bandanas were everywhere. They were bolder, and definitely louder. Joe winced as the furious amplified Spanish raked his eardrums.

A familiar face passed by.

"Hey," Joe called.

The man turned away, adjusted his New York Yankees cap and quickened his pace.

"Paulo!" Joe crashed through the crowd, grabbing his arm.

Paulo struggled for a moment then appeared surprised. Joe thought he was faking it and had tried to run past.

"Oh, hey, man," Paulo said, "what are you doing here? How you doing?"

"I'm okay. And you?"

"Busy, man. Real busy." He looked over Joe's shoulder.

"What about Nina? Is she around?"

"She's around."

"Can you give us a ride on your boat? I want to visit the Huapi with her."

"Aw. I don't know, man. She doesn't let me go there anymore. Says we were bothering them."

"She doesn't? Well, I could talk to her about that. I'd pay you, of course."

"I don't know. You can take the tour tomorrow."

"I don't want the standard tour. I want to see the Huapi. Say hi to the chief. I could pay a lot."

That seemed to catch Paulo's attention, but he held firm. "I know you can pay, buddy. Still, I don't know."

"What's the problem?"

"I think they might kill you."

Joe set down his travel bag. "Kill me? Who? Why?"

"Hasn't she called you?"

Joe said nothing.

"The scene is bad, man. It's dangerous. Nina's been trying to help, but I tell her to stay away."

"Helping them? With what? You said you didn't take her there. What's going on?"

"I don't know for sure, but it seems obvious. You took that color-stone thing, and a few months later, the Palaguans showed up to mine the cave on Huapi land. That's what caused the violence. The miners will be back for sure once they get more security. I've heard they're going to send the stone to the USA. What did you expect? Why do you look so surprised?"

Joe moaned, running his hand through his hair. All his fears about Nina's message were true.

Paulo continued. "The miners killed three young Huapi men. And the chief's son killed someone from the mining company. At least, that's what I heard from Nina."

"They told me everything was going to be cleared with the Huapi," Joe said. "That the land would pay for itself."

"And you believed them?" Paulo laughed.

"I held out until it was cleared with the Palaguan government. Four people? Murdered?" Joe's heart dropped into an abyss. He had the money to help Billy, but now others were dead.

Paulo snorted. "Everything was cleared with the Palaguan government, but not the Huapi? Man, I mean no disrespect, but are you stupid? The government here can't even pave the roads, do you really think they could negotiate on the side of the Huapi against an American multinational?"

Joe absorbed the information and felt his face burn. "I'm going to sue them when I get back to the states," he said. "Sue them hard. For now, you have to take me. With or without Nina. I have to see what's happening."

"All right, man, if you insist. We'll look for her. But before we go, you pay up just in case you don't make it back."

2

"Wait here," Paulo said as he and Joe arrived outside Nina's basement apartment.

Joe leaned against the wall and rubbed his face, his mind racing with all Paulo had said. The Huapi hated him? Three boys dead? Ndiko killed a miner? But the Palaguans said it was fine! The ambassador himself had said it was okay, it was part of the agreement. Did they mean only the Palaguans, not the Huapi? Was this all over Crystal Clay? But the MajorCo Toy execs said a deal was worked out, that they had permission!

What a fool he was! He would call his attorney, hire an army of lawyers, as soon as he could to straighten this out. He'd sue. But what if he lost the money? Then how would Billy get the best treatment?

Joe put aside his frantic angst and listened as Paulo walked deeper into Nina's place. "Miss Nina? I'm here early. I ran into someone." His voice trailed off and whispered in Spanish. Joe could hear Nina reply.

Footsteps approached. The door swung open. Nina scowled at him. "Come in," she said. "Quickly."

Joe ducked in. "What are you doing here?" she asked, her voice harsh.

"I came down to see you. And to check on the Huapi. I didn't know all of this was going on until Paulo mentioned it."

"Didn't you get my messages?"

Joe stared at his feet.

Nina pointed at him, accusing, "For thousands of years, the Huapi guard their sacred cave, then you save the Chief's life and in a fit of lunacy, he gives you a piece of their sacred crystal, the gift from the gods. Now, suddenly, this mineral, never known about by any white man for millennia, is being sought by everyone. Don't pretend you don't know what happened."

Joe looked up, but said nothing.

"Did you happen to sell it to MajorCo Toys?"

"I did, but–"

"I knew it!" she said, flinging her arms in the air. "You unbelievable idiot!"

"Wait. Wait. Don't talk to me like that. I didn't know. They said they got permission. I held out until they even brought in the Palaguan ambassador. My lawyer worked out a deal with them."

"A deal? With who?"

"I couldn't give them specifics or they just would have run in. They said whoever the native peoples were, a deal would be worked out with them. My lawyer assured me it was okay. I made them put in a clause in the contract to include the Huapi."

"And you believed him?"

"Yes. I did. They said once a deal was reached, the land would be protected forever. It would pay for itself."

"So when was this supposed to take place? Because I've been visiting with the tribe and I haven't heard about their cut of the profits, or when they will be able to buy their own land. Or if there will be any left worth buying anyway."

"I don't know. I don't know all the details."

"There's a lot you don't know. Well, here's the facts: they're all set to mine the cave, and four people are dead. Three Huapi and one worker."

"I heard."

"Well, at least you're aware of something."

"I never would have said anything if I knew this was how it would turn out. But I held out. I tried, damn it. I have it on the contract."

"Where did you think your magic crystal would come from?"

"I'm not stupid," he said to Paulo, then turned on Nina. "And I'm not naïve. I insisted there be a deal. If anything, I was lied to."

"Do you really think the Huapi gave permission for their gift from the gods to be raped? You saw how angry Ndiko was. You were drunk on money."

Joe could feel his heart racing. "Enough. Stop it. Stop this. I'm not going to take this abuse. I never intended anything wrong. As soon as I get back, I'll go straight to my lawyer and my other contacts and tell them this has to stop or there will be legal action. Should be an easy case. It's written and signed and agreed to."

"Do you really think that's going to work?"

"Why wouldn't it?"

"Oh maybe because it's a small native tribe against a massive company with infinite resources," Nina said. "What time is it?"

She looked at her watch.

"I'll head over to get things ready," Paulo said and left.

Joe closed his eyes, trying to calm his spinning thoughts. Nina dug around in a box of junk, and pulled out a small pouch full of pills.

"You want to help?" she asked Joe. "Shove this down your pants. Don't let Paulo see it."

* * *

Walking as naturally as he could with the bundle hidden in his pants, Joe followed Nina to the marina where Paulo was preparing his boat. Once they were out on the river, Paulo turned on the radio. Every station he flipped to was full of angry shouting.

"This PRM revolutionary crap is killing the music," Paulo said. "The radio is all politics all the time now. They want to complain about oppression? How about they stop oppressing the tunes, man?"

He cursed in Spanish.

Nina moved to the back of the boat with Joe.

"We'll sit back here so Paulo can't hear us," she said. "I don't tell him everything and he's just fine with that."

"What are you keeping him in the dark about?"

"Since the confrontation, when those four people were killed, the Palaguan government has set up checkpoints around the Huapi land. They want to prevent the PRM rebels from taking over the mine, or smuggling weapons through previously unwatched areas. In case you haven't noticed, things have gotten tense around here."

"I did notice. The red banners. The shouting crowds. The police."

"There are at least a dozen arrests per week. And the revolutionary movement is growing."

"But that doesn't explain what you're keeping from Paulo."

"I'm sure he knows," Nina sighed, "but I never say anything. I've been smuggling supplies to the Huapi. It's all basic stuff to you and me, but I hope it's new, life-saving convenience to them. Water-purification tablets, painkillers, dried meals, vitamins, that kind of stuff. It's easier for them to avoid the government patrols and mining area if they don't have to venture out of the village.

And it's easier for me if Paulo takes me in instead of me walking it in. What's currently riding in your pants is part of this week's batch. I just got Paulo involved. This whole project is one big improvisation."

"Where do all the supplies come from?"

"I pay for it. Friends ship stuff from the USA. The US Embassy was no help. I've contacted the usual NGOs, but so far nothing. I think they're probably overworked as it is. They can't chase every issue, there's just too many."

"I can help, too. I have money. Plenty of it."

Nina looked away. "Of course I could use it, but your money came from their suffering. To help them using the same money that came from their pain just seems wrong."

"But it's the only money I have. I'll wire you some. As much as you want. I want to make this right. I didn't mean for any of this to happen. The guys at MajorCo told me they got permission. The ambassador promised a deal. I swear!"

"I believe you."

Joe shrugged. "I should have known it was too easy."

Nina touched his knee. Her face softened. Joe hoped she might say something forgiving. She seemed about to speak when her attention was drawn over his shoulder.

"Here comes a checkpoint."

3

Paulo slowed the boat as it veered off the main waterway and into a narrow tributary. A larger ship equipped with a metal hull and mounted with guns was blocking their way. Joe cringed, knowing the large weapons could cut them to pieces in seconds, but Paulo seemed fearless. He waved and smiled enthusiastically, as if greeting old friends. Joe sat down, the bag of pills in his pants becoming more and more uncomfortable. His sweat felt like an adhesive, gluing the package to his inner thigh.

The soldiers smiled and waved back to Paulo, but the captain, easily recognized by the way his men parted to make way for him, frowned and merely nodded. He immediately pointed to Joe and began barking in Spanish.

Joe waved, his legs shaking. He was terrified what might happen if they caught him. Would he be thrown in some Palaguan jail forever? Branded a drug smuggler for something as innocent as vitamins?

The captain descended a ladder with an assistant and began inspecting the boat. He walked over to Joe and stood before him. Joe looked into the man's eyes and tried not to tremble.

The captain said something gruffly. Joe looked to Paulo and Nina.

"Stand up," Nina ordered. "He wants you to stand."

Joe did, his heart thundering in his chest, the plastic bag peeling off his skin, catching in his underwear. The captain frowned again and poked Joe in the chest, mumbling.

Joe simply replied, "Hello."

Paulo quickly came over and began laughing and chattering. Nina translated.

"He's saying you've been feeling a bit seasick."

The captain smirked scornfully at Joe, who smiled and shrugged. Paulo laughed too and clapped the captain on his back, turning him away from the sight of his men.

Joe saw Paulo transfer a roll of cash to the captain's hand in one quick motion. The roll vanished into the captain's pocket. Paulo stepped away and the captain spun to exit the boat. It was a beautifully choreographed and well-practiced move. Beyond relief, Joe felt a sort of awe, in the presence of two true masters in the art of bribery.

The police boat slid to the side, letting them pass. Joe waved as they went by. His wave was not returned.

"See?" Nina said to him. "Paulo knows what he's doing."

"Obviously," Joe said, shifting to adjust his pants.

4

Paulo guided the ashore on the same beach where Joe had saved Chief Maubombo's life. Ndiko was standing there waiting, somber and alone, an empty sack thrown over his shoulder.

"What is he doing here?" he pointed toward Joe as Nina handed him a package of basic supplies concealed in the boat's compartments. Paulo looked up and down the river, scanning for police.

"He's asking what you are doing here," Nina said to Joe coldly.

Joe stammered. "I… uh… um… came here to bring good wishes." He fished the package out of his pants and handed it to Nina as she translated his words to Huapi.

Ndiko snorted, "The pales have already brought their machines. They prepare to steal our gift from the gods. He has his share. Why should he be here?"

Nina translated but Joe did not reply.

Once all the goods had been stuffed into Ndiko's sack, he and Nina conversed in Huapi while Joe sat by, rudely ignored. Paulo's head kept swiveling back and forth, watching up and down the river, tapping a salsa beat on the boat's wheel. The sun's heat pressed down on them all.

"How are things?" Nina asked Ndiko.

"The same. No one wants to venture out for fear of being killed. So we drink the dirty water that runs through our village. Most stay away from the sacred cave so there is no more bloodshed."

Nina nodded, frowning.

"Oh, one more thing," Ndiko said. "The chief is dying."

"Your father?"

"Yes."

"Of what?"

"Cowardice. He promised his father that he would not witness the end of our people. But now the pales are coming. He thinks the end is near, so he has given up his will to live, in order to fulfill his promise."

Nina sat down. "My God," she said in English.

"What? What's happening?" Joe asked.

"The chief. He's dying."

Ndiko flicked his hand towards Joe and said, "It is as if this man is my father's murderer. But then if I truly believed that I would strangle his tiny pale neck with my bare hands. My father was a fool to give away the gift. He has left me with this legacy. I've lost the strength to hate this man. For now."

"What is he saying about me?" Joe asked, irritated.

Nina ignored him and asked Ndiko, "I'm not a doctor, but I'll try to find someone who can help. Maybe I can bring medicines to help him."

Ndiko thought about it. "Don't bother. He doesn't want that."

"I'd like, I mean, do you think he'd mind, if I, um, said thank you… and goodbye?"

"You are welcome to visit him." Ndiko slung the pack of supplies over his shoulder, inclining his head toward Joe. "And you may bring him also."

"I'm going," Nina said, as she leapt over the side of the boat.

Joe followed her. "What? Why? What's happening?"

"Whoa, wait a minute," Paulo said. "This isn't part of the plan. This was just a drop-off."

"I'll be back soon," Nina said to him. "The chief is dying. I'm going to say goodbye. Joe, you're welcome to come, too."

"What should I do?" he asked, hating how pathetic he sounded.

"Whatever you want."

Joe looked back at Paulo, who was shaking his head. "Nina, the trouble you cause me. Just be quick."

Joe followed Nina and Ndiko into the jungle.

5

Joe was stunned by the contrast. The small village once full of smiles and activity was now populated with shuffling, fearful people. Instead of rushing to greet him, the Huapi clutched at those nearby, warning them to stay back, keep away from the pale ones. The frightened gazes followed their every move.

Ndiko led on. Some children greeted Nina. She smiled at their familiar faces. They watched Joe warily. He could tell that some of them recognized him, but they said nothing. Anger or fear, most likely both, burned in their eyes.

"My father dies in there," Ndiko said, pointing to a hut. He then turned away, carrying the sack to another hut, where he was met by the bulk of the tribe seeking supplies.

Joe stayed close to Nina as she pushed aside the curtain made from leaves and stepped slowly into the darkness.

Paulo's words rang in his head: "They might kill you."

A Huapi woman collided with them on her way out, sobbing uncontrollably.

Am I walking to my own death, or someone else's? Joe wondered.

A low boom sounded in the distance. It sounded odd, as though muted. Nina looked around, confused.

"Something at the mine? Or thunder?" Joe said.

Nina didn't respond. They both lowered their heads in reverence.

Yuala knelt by the thatch bedside of her husband, gently stroking his hand, her proud face streaked with tears.

Joe could feel his own pulse hammering inside his head.

A ragged voice spoke from the bed through the darkness.

Nina looked away, sobbing.

"Nina. Please," Joe said. "What is the chief saying?"

She translated. "He said if you've come here, you can't be all evil."

Joe tried to swallow the lump in his throat, but somehow it stayed in place. He closed his eyes tight but tears still got through.

The thunder outside grew. The ground shook. Frightened voices of the Huapi yelled across the village.

"Is that an earthquake?" Joe asked. The hairs on the back of his neck stood up.

Nina ignored him and together they knelt at the side of Chief Maubombo's deathbed. The chief's round face was slack and bulbous, instead of taken up by his giant smile.

The chief placed his withered hand on Joe's knee. The dying man's fingers felt like dried sticks being laid gently across leg. Joe spoke first.

"Chief. I am sorry. I didn't know."

Nina translated.

The chief spoke with great effort, mumbling. "I gave you a gift, now your kind comes for it and you say you didn't know. That is worse than doing this to me with hatred."

Joe nodded.

"I didn't know. If…"

The chief (through Nina) interrupted him. "I have no more time. But I have one request."

"I will right this, I will stop it."

"Silence. One request."

"Anything," Joe said, swallowing his tears. "I will work my lifetime for it."

The chief's lips trembled as he gathered precious air to speak with. "As I was dying. I heard you. I don't speak your language, but I knew what you were saying. You were begging me to return, cursing me to come back."

"Yes," Joe said. "I did."

"And all I ask you now is, if you are truly not evil, then let me die. Don't save me this time. Don't let me witness the coming desecration."

Joe cleared his throat as quietly as he could. "I will let you die."

The chief turned his head away. Nina hugged Yuala tenderly.

"I promise. I will stop this," Joe said, his voice cracking. Nina translated.

Maubombo formed a trembling grin.

"So many foolish promises," he gasped.

6

Before Joe could reply, there was a scuffle outside the hut. Someone was pushing their way in. Joe put his head down and didn't move. He thought it might be Ndiko come to kill him, but he didn't care. Guilt and the chief's words made him feel so heavy he couldn't move. He wasn't sure he wanted to live anymore anyway.

"Nina! Nina!"

It was Paulo, calling frantically.

Nina whirled around. "Have respect! Be quiet. What is it?"

"On the radio," Paulo said. "The PRM rebels, they're attacking the airfield! The prime minister has been killed. A revolution is underway." The thunder sounded again, this time close enough to reveal its true nature: mortar attacks on Palagua City. Paulo's eyes darted in all directions.

"We should get out of here," he whispered. "There's no telling what might happen."

Nina grabbed Joe's hand and pulled him from the hut. Joe looked over his shoulder in time to see Yuala staring out at the three of them. The light outside snapped Joe free from his trance. He turned, running with Nina behind Paulo.

The boat ride back to Palagua city was bumpy. Paulo whipped his boat around the sharp bends in the river with one hand, tuning the radio for updates with the other. Every station was filled with revolutionary bluster, raised to a frantic pitch. Where the police checkpoint had been before, there was only the burning wreckage of a boat. The arrogant captain's corpse was slung over one side of the listing vessel.

"Oh, no," Paulo snarled, tuning the radio again. The voices were angry and merciless.

The boat hit the marina dock, barely slowing, nearly catapulting them out.

"What's the plan?" Joe asked.

"The plan is you get off my boat," Paulo said. His quick hands went to work. By loosening a few knots on his boat's identifying streamers, the Palaguan flag vanished, and the red banner of the revolution appeared in its place. Paulo pulled a red bandana from his pocket and began waving it above his head, joining a passing throng of celebrating revolutionary supporters, all waving rags of red.

"I'm heading back to my apartment," Nina said. "You should get out of here now or you might not ever. They might be looking for Americans. Bargaining chips as hostages, black market passports, money. Who knows?"

Joe slung his bag over his shoulder.

"Drop everything except the most important stuff," Nina reminded him. "In case you need to run."

Joe set the bag down and kept only his wallet and passport. "Lead the way."

"In case we get separated, keep working your way to the airport. Head to the east. It's almost evening, so move away from the sun."

They darted from the marina, where a giant explosion had demolished a Palaguan tour boat. Flames blackened the colorful mermaids painted on the hull, and singed the still dolphins.

"Get home," Joe said. "I'll go alone. When I get back, I'll send word. And I'm going to put a stop-" His sentence was cut off by a whistling sound as a mortar destroyed a fruit stand down the street. Warm dust rushed over them.

"Go!" he yelled. Nina nodded grimly and ran off toward her apartment. Joe sprinted in the opposite direction, heading for the airport.

* * *

The streets alternated between emptiness and debris. Leaving the marina, the only people around were a few bodies in the street, limping or crawling, leaving blood trails in the dirt. Joe wanted to help, but he knew he had to get out. Plus, his last act of kindness in Palagua had unfolded into this nightmare.

Around the corner, a crowd parted, surrounding a young couple. They were tourists, judging by their Hawaiian shirts. They were desperately trying to fend off the blows raining down on them. Finally, a man with a police officer's jacket and cut-off shorts fired a shot in the air. The crowd pushed the young couple against a wall, and ran back. The officer lined up riflemen in front of them as the couple stroked each other's face, crying.

Joe turned to run, but he was already found.

A staggering Palaguan stood before him, a knife in his shaking hand.

"Americano? Tú americano?" the man said.

Joe stepped to the side. The man grinned and mirrored his movement, blocking his way.

This could be it, Joe thought as he faked searching for his wallet. This could be where I die. His heart shriveled into a cold, crumpled thing. Survival was all that mattered now.

"Dinero," the Palaguan said. "Dinero." He lunged with the knife.

Joe dodged to the side, dropped his shoulder, charged and swung upward, redirecting the blade. His palm connected with the thief's jaw, crushing it with a satisfying crack. A lightning bolt of pain from the impact shot down his arm, but Joe roared and kept running, his feet churning. He knocked the man to the ground, stomped on his face and sprinted away, not looking back until he was out of breath. The thief had not followed.

In the distance, he could see the entrance of the airport. A tank squatted in the grass, soldiers lined either side of the terminal. Black smoke boiled from behind the building.

Joe waited and watched as a car sputtered to the front. Three men in suits jumped out, holding their arms high, passports displayed in their right hands. The soldiers aimed their guns at them, but seeing them to be no threat, waved them into the terminal.

Joe bolted from his hiding place, imitating the three businessmen before him.

"I'm American! American! Estados Unidos!" he yelled, holding his passport open, hands above his head. The soldiers nearest him raised their guns and aimed at him.

"Estados Unidos! I'm American!" he shouted again.

"Hurry! Hurry!" A woman called from the entrance, holding open the door.

Joe ran to her.

"Are there any flights left?" he gasped.

"Only one and only to Los Angeles," she answered. Joe emptied his wallet onto the counter.

"Will that cover it?"

An explosion from the runway blew in a whole section of the terminal's windows. Silver snow rained onto the sea shell-patterned rug.

"Forget the money. You may have to stand," the woman said. "Now go." She pointed him across the terminal, across the field of recently shattered glass.

I have to walk into that war zone? Joe wondered to himself. He clenched his fists and forced himself to move forward.

As he crossed the patterned carpet, among the fake palm trees, he looked over his shoulder. The front of the terminal was serene, completely calm and ordinary, except for the soldiers and tank guarding it. The back of the terminal, where he was heading, was a battle-torn ruin. The transition from well-armed tourist paradise to battlefield hell occurred in a matter of steps.

He opened the door leading to the tarmac.

A soldier yanked him out, grabbed the back of his head and pushed him down. "Cabeza abajo!"

The soldier knelt next to him and pointed toward the boarding stairs leading to the plane. Joe nodded understanding. Salvation was a 100-yard dash away.

Two other soldiers nearby dropped to their knees and nodded to Joe, creating a virtual path with the barrels of their machine guns.

Government forces darted back and forth underneath the plane, using the landing gear as cover, exchanging fire with the rebels emerging from the jungle along the runway.

Someone shoved Joe aside and waved his passport. Joe recognized the flag of Japan on the cover.

"Solamente americanos!" one soldier said and shoved the intruder back.

"But I speak American!" the man yelled. "I am American businessman!"

The soldier spun his gun and shoved the butt into the man's belly. The man fell over, curling up. He pulled out his wallet, offering the colored plastic to the soldiers. The soldiers kicked him until he slunk away, back into the terminal.

The lead soldier put his hand on Joe's chest, holding him back. He held up three fingers.

"En tres."

He signaled to the other two.

They replied, "Sí."

"We cover you," the leader said to Joe in English. Joe nodded and dropped to a sprinter's block start.

"Uno."

Bullet holes traced a dotted course across the side of the plane.

"Dos."

A rebel stepped from the jungle and was gunned down, falling backward.

"Tres!"

The soldiers stepped from their cover and fired. Flashes erupted from the brush. Joe leapt out onto the blacktop, feeling terribly open, more naked than he had ever felt. He bolted, hunched over, using his arms to cover his head.

"Just keep moving," he repeated to himself. "Just keep moving." Gravel exploded at his feet.

He was up the stairs and into the plane.

Muzzle flashes erupted from the jungle.

A woman in the second row screamed as her window cracked, a bullet lodged in the glass.

A flight attendant shoved Joe into the front seat and lifted the stairs as the plane started rolling.

"Let's get out of here!" someone yelled.

Outside, Joe saw the Japanese man running toward the plane, waving for it to stop. Bullets cut him down as the attendant closed the door.

The small plane was already lifting. An overhead luggage compartment blew open, spilling clothes everywhere.

Over all the chaos, Joe fumbled with his seat belt. He could hear a frantic chattering from the cabin, "R-P-G! R-P-G!" the plane lifted and banked sickeningly to the right. Through the tiny window, Joe saw the rebels running onto the end of the runway, advancing from the jungle. One had a shoulder-fired rocket launcher.

With helpless horror, Joe watched him kneel and fire.

The rocket sped toward the plane, right at his window.

The plane's wing sliced through the smoky white column left by the rocket.

"Missed!" he yelled, ecstatic, insane.

A muffled explosion shook the aircraft. Oxygen masks dropped from the ceiling and the lights went out. The plane's engine choked. Wheezed. The nose tilted downward.

They all held their breath, sitting in the darkness, too terrified to make a noise. Joe counted six seconds and a thousand beats of his heart.

The lights came back on, and the engines roared, awakening.

The crippled plane lifted over the jungle and into the sky.

Some were hysterically crying, some muttering prayers to their god or their cell phones.

Joe stared out the window. The jungle disappeared behind clouds beneath him. Soon all he could see from his window was the wing, its front edge blackened from the rocket's explosion.

He didn't blink for several minutes.

7

"Billy!" Teri called. "Pick up the phone, it's Joe!"

Billy bounded down the hall and lifted the handset in his bedroom.

"Hey, rich man," Teri said on the phone from the kitchen. "World traveler. How have you been? I've been thinking about you."

Joe's voice was low, guarded. "I'm okay, I guess. Things haven't been going well. Have you heard about Palagua on the news?"

"Are you all right?"

"I'm okay. What about the news?"

"There was a ten-second blurb on the morning shows. I was worried, but they said no Americans were known to be in danger. Something about a rebellion, a pro-democracy government throwing out the communists."

Joe sighed loudly. "I don't know about those labels. Whoever is in power is going to mine the Huapi land until it's barren."

"I've been doing some research," Billy said, his voice low. "I found a website that was talking about how some Huapi were killed."

Joe's voice cracked. Teri felt his anguish through the phone before he composed himself.

"Yes, a miner was killed too," he said. "Somehow we have to tell people what's going on before more of them want Crystal Clay."

He paused for a long time.

"Joe?" Teri asked. "You still there? Joe?"

Finally Joe said, "Sorry, Ace, I didn't get you a piece like I promised."

"You didn't?" Billy asked.

"No. I'm sorry."

Teri held her breath.

"Well," Billy sighed heavily. "I guess that's okay. I don't want it if it's going to mess up the Huapi's land."

Joe hesitated again. "Teri, that's a great kid you've got there. You're a good man, Billy."

"So what are you going to do now?" Teri asked.

"Anything and everything I can in every way I can. Legal, media, you name it. I've already hooked up with an agent."

"An agent? But you just got back."

"I have to act fast. Look, I have to go, she's on the other line. I'll be in touch, okay?"

He hung up.

Teri trudged upstairs to her son's room.

Billy was lying in bed, his lamp on, reading. He frowned, partly concentrating, partly sad. Teri patted his chest and pulled the covers up to his neck. She removed the bandana from his head and ran her hand over his hairless scalp.

"Everyone at school wants Crystal Clay," he said, setting his book aside.

"Do you?"

"No. Not anymore. The one Joe gave me was cool because it didn't have some dumb shape like the ones on the commercials. It was different. Cory's bragging about how he's already pre-ordered a million of them. Some girl said she's going to make a sculpture with them."

"You sure you don't want one?"

"Yeah. I only wanted the one Joe gave me at first. Now, it's not the same."

She nodded.

"Mom, do you think he'll be coming to visit us again?"

"I don't know, honey. He said he has lots to take care of."

"No he doesn't. He quit his job. He told us."

"Well, now he has something else to do. He's going to stop Crystal Clay."

"No he's not. I just told you everyone wants it. He's acting weird. I hate that he's rich."

"Sometimes money changes people."

"I don't care if he doesn't bring back the Crystal Clay he gave me. I just want to hang out with him again. Watch some movies, have pizza. Like we used to."

"I know. But he's still Joe, right?"

"Not the Joe I like." Billy said, lifting his book. He was reading a high school-level text about mythology.

Teri stood up to leave.

"Maybe Joe is a myth," her son said. "Someone I just made up, so I could live through him, go to distant places, have adventures."

"No, Billy, he's real. That's the problem. Just give him a chance, okay?"

"Okay." His eyes turned to his book.

"Did you take your meds?"

Billy turned the empty cup on his nightstand so she could see it. She kissed his head and went to her bedroom.

Teri stared at the dark ceiling, breathing deeply, willing her heart not to break for her son, and hoping it wouldn't harden towards Joe.

8

"Check out this segment. It's our latest canned news report," the head of MajorCo Toys marketing said, pushing a button on the remote control. The television showed a reporter standing in a mall in front of a MajorCo toy store. She was wearing a Santa cap, the pom-pom flopped over one eye.

"During our hot toy preview this year, the undisputed king of Christmas is sure to be Crystal Clay, a collectible of several basic shapes from MajorCo Toys. What makes this gift so attractive are the bright colors that scatter off it like a disco ball or a prism. Even in the dark! And it doesn't need external light or batteries."

She held the piece of Crystal Clay up to the camera.

"I was allowed to see an early, raw version of the toy. It's beautiful, isn't it? Despite the name, the clay is not flexible, but children in pre-market testing are going crazy for them. My kids are already working on their letters to Santa. Now, back to the news desk."

The room erupted in applause just as Joe crashed in.

The team fell silent.

Joe scanned the walls. They were covered with ad campaign ideas promoting Crystal Clay.

"What's wrong?" someone asked. "You look like you've been through a war zone."

"I have. I just got back from Palagua," he growled.

"The land that fed us all. How is it down there?"

Ethan Scherr rose from his seat and slapped Joe on the shoulder.

"Hey, buddy. I thought you might stop by. Worried about the news? Don't be. I hear they promised doubled their agreed-upon output. There was a bit of a scare with the revolution, but it turns out the new government is facing reality and willing to play ball. They're moving real fast. Our bread and butter is safe."

"Good thing," one of the marketers said. "Last thing we would need is Palagua going all Cuba on us."

"I was there," Joe said, shrugging free of Ethan. "People died during that revolution and people died because of the mining of Crystal Clay. More will die unless we stop this. We have to end this mistake."

The room was uneasily quiet for a minute.

Ethan spoke first. "You were there? Palagua?"

"Died?" someone else whimpered.

Joe continued.

"They were murdered. Are being murdered. It's war. The Huapi people, the Palaguans, foreigners. The Crystal Clay is on Huapi sacred land. They call it a gift from the gods and when they tried to stop the miners, they were shot. That's not even counting how many died in the revolution. This is exactly what I wanted to prevent!"

Everyone in the room looked at each other, unsure what to say. Only Scherr spoke. "Calm down, Joe. Let's talk."

"Talk? No. No talk. The forces in Palagua are fighting over the prize. And the prize is created by our demand. So this has to stop. All of it. We have to stop marketing Crystal Clay."

Ethan chuckled uncomfortably. "You can't be serious. We've got tons of it on pre-order. Stockholders. Children waiting for Christmas. The product isn't even out yet. We're still in the hype phase."

"That's not more important than people's lives." Joe felt himself shaking but he didn't try to fight it.

"Oh, please," Ethan countered, "I've heard this all before with the sneakers and the sweatshops. This is old news. If there's a problem, we'll fix it. The last thing we want is bad public relations."

"The only way to fix it is to end it," Joe said.

"But you made a mint off of this toy. And you didn't have to do anything. It's not even in stores yet. When it does hit, let me tell you, the money's only going up."

"I don't care. I held out for a reason. This is a violation of the contract. The Huapi were to be in agreement. I'll sue. I'll stop you. I'll destroy this company."

The room was completely silent as the marketing team looked to the floor or out the window.

Only Scherr confronted Joe. "Our deal was with the old government. Our CEO went to great lengths and personal risk to make arrangements with the new government very quickly. I don't think the new arrangement included all the bells and whistles you wanted."

"People's lives are not bells and whistles."

"Let me ask you this, then. If you're so against it all, why not give your money back?"

Joe didn't answer. He didn't expect this much resistance, or this much confusion. If he gave up his money, Billy would have to go back to standard treatment. Was that a price he could accept? He was on the verge of screaming and trashing the place. He needed to think. He stormed out.

Whispers buzzed around the room.

Ethan Scherr closed the door quietly, smiling as he sat down. "Now maybe I'll never have to see that fool again," he said out loud. Spattered chuckles filled the room.

Scherr continued, "Why do you all look so depressed? That was a good sign. Only trends with real potential have a backlash. We're barely out of the gate here and we're already taking fire. Better get used to it, people. It's the price of success."

9

"To a new Palagua!" the general shouted, raising his pistol above his head and firing a single shot into the air. The miners around him cheered while soldiers kept their guns aimed into the jungle, watching for any attacking Huapi, or any remnants of the government forces. The bulldozers and drills roared to life and began their penetration of the mountain.

The cheerful atmosphere was broken by one young soldier firing several shots into the bush. After some tense moments, he and several companions closed on his target, where they discovered it was just a (now perforated) tree monkey.

The mining had begun again.

Later, under a tent halfway between the mine and Palagua City, safe from the heat and noise of either site, the general shared champagne with other dignitaries. He looked across the small skyline, where several columns of smoke were dissolving, the signs of fighting recently ended.

"The first shipment goes out tonight. We're going to be rich," the new ambassador told the assembled Palaguans. "The Americans are more frantic about getting this crystal than they are their precious drugs."

The general laughed and the new ambassador continued.

"Poor Galeno. My predecessor, God rest his soul, was playing hardball with the Americans, holding out for a higher price. I say let's mine it all and sell it for all it is worth. Palaguan pride has its place, but so does money!"

He was applauded by everyone in the tent.

"I'm glad to see you all agree," he said.

"That's why we're here and not out there, against the wall," the general laughed. Some laughed uncomfortably with him. Some simply nodded and stared at their feet.

Regardless of their actions, and the general's lack of decorum, they all knew it was true, and they all agreed.

BOOK II

Part 8

1

The trucks rumbled back and forth between Huapi land and Palagua City all night. Armed security guards marched along the road in packs, always scanning the forest. Vehicles and boots covered with debris, oil and dirt constantly splashed through the creek that supplied the Huapi with drinking water.

This was the daily reality following the Palaguan revolution. The new government was doing away with the restraint of the previous administration. Day and night, the mountain vibrated as its interior was forcefully cracked and pried loose before being shuttled away.

At first, the Huapi countered the situation by stuffing folded leaves in their ears. That cut down the overwhelming noise, but made their ear canals itch terribly. The smell of the vehicles' exhaust was countered with rolled-up leaves plugging their nostrils. That helped a little, but then their throats were burning.

When their eyes turned red, the natural remedies ran out. The children cried non-stop. Only the eye drops Nina had smuggled in helped at all, but there was never enough for everyone.

The water-purification tablets were no longer having their effect. The water had changed from clear to a muddy, slick brown. Everyone in the village could count on a bout of vomiting or diarrhea at least once a day. Even adults were no longer able to get to the downriver latrine quickly enough. The stench of human waste permanently hung about the village.

Daily tasks of hunting small game and gathering fruit were slowly scaled back. A chunk of Huapi land was cut off by the new road. None of the tribe dared cross it or come near it for fear of being shot on sight.

Less food was coming in because no one had the strength to collect it and that simply made them weaker which made them unable to hunt or gather food. That cruel cycle was accentuated by the poison air and the sickness all around.

The village was withering away.

Ndiko, as new chief, tried to do everything. He worked himself to exhaustion, leading groups as far as he could into the forest to hunt for animals that were once all around them. Every day he burned with hate, and at night, he couldn't sleep due to the noise and his rage.

"What has become of us?" someone asked him. Daily he encountered the same question, "What is your plan, great chief?"

He no longer attempted to answer in any meaningful way. "We live each day as best we can," became his only reply.

"Why not get your pale woman friend to bring us more help?" someone asked sarcastically. Those nearby shrunk back, but Ndiko's famous temper did not flare. He was too tired to respond.

As the days wore on, the tribe became nocturnal, moving about when the waves of trucks were less frequent and flood lights lanced the foliage. Sitting around a fire, the hysteria among the adults grew.

"Can't we move somewhere else?"

"Where?" Ndiko replied. "Where could we go? The city surrounds us now."

"We are all going to die."

Yuala spoke out. "That is true. We are all going to die. But if we leave our land, what will we become? That would be like killing ourselves."

"Can we fight them?"

Everyone nodded no. "That's already been tried," Ndiko said. "Their weapons are too powerful."

Yuala patted her son's shoulder and addressed the circle. "Life runs its course. Perhaps the time of the Huapi and our land has ended."

"You say that so easily, but what is my child supposed to eat and drink?" a woman wailed, her arm around an emaciated boy.

"He will live from the Huapi land, as we always have," Ndiko replied angrily.

"But there is no Huapi land," she cried. The boy moaned. The mother turned away, cooing over him. A truck in the distance blared its horn and rumbled off toward Palagua City.

A crowd of children had gathered outside the entrance to the MajorCo toy store.

"I want it! I want it! I have to have it!" the children shouted, echoing the kids they had seen in the commercials.

"Hooray, hooray for Crystal Clay! There's color in every day with Crystal Clay!"

Pimply teen stock workers unlocked the doors and stepped aside, letting the charging herd through onto the polished floors of the MajorCo Toys store.

Outside, vehicles prowled the parking lot slowly, looking for any opening among the plowed snow and other cars. Drivers shouted to each other as they hunted.

"You gonna move your car or sit there all day?"

"It's my parking spot. I was here first!"

"How about I move your car for you?"

The SUV rear-ended the sedan and pushed it over a concrete barrier. When the SUV dropped in reverse, its bumper hooked on the stuck sedan and tore off. Security guards came rushing over.

The multicultural kids pictured on the giant banner at the front of the store smiled down on the Christmas shopping chaos.

"Collect 'em all," the sign read. "Lots of different, fun-filled shapes!"

Each child held a Crystal Clay medallion in a different form: a star, a circle, a square. Each simple shape cast a rainbow-colored shadow.

Inside the store, like a time-lapse film of ants devouring an insect piece by piece, the pile of Crystal Clay toys diminished under the frantic swarm of shoppers.

"I'm sorry, we're all out of Crystal Clay," the store manager said for the hundredth time, as he stood next to a sign written in jagged letters with black magic marker. The sign's rough text said, "Crystal Clay completely out of stock."

"But I just saw a delivery truck in the back!"

At the store's loading bay, the stock team, bound up in winter clothes, emerged from the back of an 18-wheeler to face a mob of angry shoppers tearing off the tops of boxes recently unloaded.

When the looters saw the new boxes arriving, they converged on the crew.

"Is there more Crystal Clay in there?"

"We don't know what's in any of these boxes."

"Can I look at some of the others?"

The crew shrugged at each other as the shoppers invaded the back of the truck and began slicing open boxes with their keys. The store manager was called.

"Get out of here before I call security," he yelled.

The shoppers ignored him except for shouting back an occasional "Whatever" or "Just a minute." Some launched into speeches about customers always being right.

"Fine," the manager said. Instead of making good on his threat, he smugly watched the shoppers open each box, only to reveal what he already knew.

No more Crystal Clay was in this shipment.

3

In a skyscraper high above the early days of the Christmas rush overtaking the city, Ethan Scherr and the MajorCo Toys executive team surveyed the projector-screen presentation.

"This is just the beginning," the CEO said. "Item One. All Crystal Clay sold out. Item Two. Crystal Clay mentioned as 'the hot toy this Christmas' on all major TV Christmas specials."

The room was filled with applause.

"Oh, yes, and I almost forgot," he continued, with mock forgetfulness, "Item Three." He advanced to the next slide, a cartoon rocket ship was leaving the earth far behind.

"Our stock went up."

The room buzzed.

"I won't tell you by how much," he laughed. "I'll just say it doubled."

The buzzing reached a fever pitch, accentuated by clapping.

"That's right. However much money you had in MajorCo Toys, multiply it by two. And we're just getting started."

The cheering rivaled a New Year's Eve party.

The CEO looked approvingly across the thunderous celebration. He caught Ethan Scherr's eye and winked.

4

Joe's hands were sweating and his mouth was dry, but he didn't drink more than a sip of bottled water. Worse than being thirsty would be having to take a leak during his speech.

He needed courage. He thought of Chief Maubombo's final words. "Don't save me this time," the chief had said, gazing up with dying eyes. Joe breathed deeply to calm his pounding heart. It didn't work, but he had to do this, not just for Maubombo but for all the Huapi.

That's why you hired a public relations firm, he interjected into his racing thoughts.

"That's why you have an agent," he whispered aloud, "What was her name again? Who cares? She is welcoming reporters to your news conference because of the Huapi and the Huapi are the reason you are getting ready to go against the same people who made you rich. You have to summon the courage."

"Don't save me this time," Joe said. Only the chief's plea kept him from bolting from the stage fright.

His attention focused as his press agent took to the podium and concluded her opening statements.

"I'd like to introduce you to the man who brought the now-famous Crystal Clay to America, who has courageously risked his financial stake in MajorCo toys after witnessing the death and destruction in Palagua firsthand. A man of integrity determined to do what is right. Mister Joe Vera."

Joe strode to the stage amidst some polite applause and camera flashes. He looked into the lights and spoke before he could think about it too much.

"Good afternoon. My name is Joe Vera. Not long ago, I was on a vacation in Palagua, where the Huapi tribe, who have occupied their small parcel of land on the edge of Palagua City for thousands of years, honored me by showing me a cave that contained what they called their gift from the gods..."

He told his story: from rags to riches in under five minutes.

"Today, I am calling on all Americans to do what is right. Boycott MajorCo Toys and Crystal Clay. Do not support the annihilation of this sacred land and these innocent people. Please. Three Huapi and one Palaguan have already been killed in clashes, and the revolution has caused countless other deaths. The new Palaguan government has started to mine again, further jeopardizing the Huapi men, women and children. Please, I urge you, do not shop at MajorCo Toys. Until they stop shipping the Crystal Clay toys. Now I'll take some questions."

"Mister Vera, isn't it true you've made a fortune off Crystal Clay?"

"I've made a fortune on the advance that MajorCo toys paid me. Yes. And I am putting as much of that money as I can toward pressuring them to stop marketing Crystal Clay."

"Will you give the money back, if they agree to stop the mining?"

Joe's agent had prepared him for that one. "I have fulfilled my end of our agreement. I deserve to keep the money. Instead of giving it to MajorCo, I will use it to help the Huapi." His agent - what was her name again? - gave him a thumbs-up from the back of the room.

"But don't you think-"

"Please recall that I attempted to have protections for the Huapi written into my original agreement with MajorCo Toys. I even had a verbal assurance from the late Palaguan ambassador, Manuel Carlos Galeno. My legal team is pursuing that angle, but we don't hold much hope for it, as the agreement was made with the previous government. That's why, with your help, I'm going to the source, the American consumer. Use your dollars to make a difference."

"But Mister Vera, what about the jobs created by this mining? Palagua is seeing an influx of money such as they never have before. Don't you think that's good?"

"Not at the expense of the native peoples."

"Is this just a publicity stunt to get more people interested in Crystal Clay?"

He could see his agent roll her eyes from the back of the room. She nodded approval as Joe responded tersely, "Absolutely not."

Joe felt himself becoming more comfortable with each question. Finally, there were no more raised hands and nothing more to say. An hour had passed in what felt like a minute.

"Anyone else?" he asked, relieved that no one responded.

"If I could just say some final words," he said. "Long ago, when our ancestors came to America, there was a great genocide. A great wrong was done. But that is past and there is nothing we can do about it today. This is something we can prevent, and we can do so easily. Boycott Crystal Clay!"

He raised his fist for the photo opportunity, just as he and his agent had practiced early this morning. He held the pose for several camera flashes, then stepped down. His mouth was chapped and cracking. He was shaking.

His agent took the podium. "Thank you for your time. If you need any more information, please contact me at the numbers in your press packets. Please, don't buy Crystal Clay. Boycott MajorCo toys until they stop their oppression of the Huapi. Thank you."

5

Joe answered his phone the morning after his news conference.

"Vera?" the caller asked.

"Scherr?"

"Yeah, it's me," Ethan Scherr said. "Joe, are you okay?"

"No. I'm mad. I feel lied to and betrayed. Before you say anything else, let me repeat, I want you to stop taking the Crystal Clay."

"Look, Joe. I'm calling you because you're all over the news. I read all about your press conference from six different sources. This is insane, man. We both stand to make a lot more money here. I want you to end this foolishness now."

"I want the same from you."

"Damn it, Joe. We waited on all your demands. We went through the Palaguan government. What more do you want? They don't have a problem with it."

"But the Huapi do."

"We can't get permission from every single person in the world, Joe."

"They live on that land."

"But they technically don't own it. It's legally designated a reservation."

"You've got to stop Crystal Clay, Ethan."

"Well, why can't they just move?"

"Why can't you just stop?"

"Come on, Joe. Be reasonable. You know the way the world is. Christmas is coming. It's going to be MajorCo's biggest year ever. If it wasn't us, it would be someone else. It's out of both of our hands now. I couldn't stop it even if I wanted to."

"You've. Got. To. Stop. It. Now."

"Sorry."

"People died."

"Joe, I'm human. Remember? Do you think I'm glad about that? Nobody wants to hurt the natives, and nobody is trying to hurt them. Of course the deaths are regrettable, but we need to move on. And since I seem to need to keep repeating it, I will. We've gotten the okay from the government. It's all legal."

"But it's not right. You haven't gotten the okay from the people who live there."

"We got it from the Palaguans. They're the ones who own that land, not the-"

"Scherr, you're an idiot."

"I'm an idiot? Of all the people I've made millionaires, you're the most ungrateful."

"I have no doubt about that."

"MajorCo will cut your pay."

"Fine. I'll sue."

"You'll lose."

They both hung up at the same time.

Joe chuckled as he rose from bed. "That went well," he snorted.

He checked his answering machine. "Joe. Sheldon Mora. Your lawyer and representative. Remember me? I have to tell you, your little blow-up at the MajorCo meeting the other day has caused some problems. So did that news conference I advised you against. I know it was in the fine print, but part of the agreement you signed is that you wouldn't speak out against MajorCo Toys. And if you did, payments would stop."

Sheldon cleared his throat.

"Which is exactly what they're threatening to do. Now the money you've earned so far, that will be tough for them to get, don't worry about that. It's the future that concerns me. They aren't thrilled about the way you've been acting. Call me. Joe, you're throwing away a lot of money."

Joe grabbed the answering machine and hurled it across the room.

6

Nina stayed low to the ground, creeping through the white haze in the jungle. The rumbling noise of the trucks hid any sound she might make so she needed only to worry about being seen. She might have admired the eerie sunrise, the mist lanced by beams of light, if the fumes from the mining didn't scorch her nose with its stink.

The further into the jungle she moved, the more intense the odor. The Huapi village couldn't be far now, she told herself.

She clutched a satchel full of supplies. This was her third solo delivery in as many weeks. She had to go alone. Paulo was skittish after the close call during the revolution.

Nina always set out as early as possible, before the full complement of miners arrived, when the area was thinly patrolled by security guards.

She jolted when someone nearby spoke.

"Hello. Nice to see you again."

She froze, until she realized the language was Huapi. She spun around, looking every direction, startled as Ndiko dropped from a tree.

"You are so unlike the women of my tribe," he said. "They weep at our fate. Even my own mother, though to others she speaks bravely. But you, you are strong, defiant."

Nina didn't like the way he was acting. He staggered as if he was tipsy. She knew chewing too much of the tree bark could cause that.

"You make it sound like I'm almost as good as a man," she said sarcastically.

"Yes," Ndiko said, not smiling, "but you're more like..." He paused, searching for the Huapi words: "A double-woman." He reached to touch her. She smacked his hand away.

"In my village, that would be close to blasphemy."

"And don't you forget it."

His eyes flew open in surprise as he laughed bitterly. She stepped away from him.

"So, your women weep?" she asked, changing the subject.

Ndiko leaned back against a tree and stared up at the forest canopy while he spoke. "The women in my tribe weep and do little more. The men yell at them for weeping and do nothing else. We dare not confront the pales. We barely venture out, moving only when it is near dark, for basic food. The noise rattles our bones, the stench stings our eyes and noses. The water is poison, but no one fights. No one wants a sudden death, so we settle for a slow one."

"Are the supplies I bring helping?"

He turned his head from staring up to look at her. Nina did not like the crazed look in his watery eyes. She was suddenly very eager to go home.

She handed him her satchel and watched as he rummaged through it.

"Is there anything else you want?" she asked.

He frowned at the pouch. "Now I feel like one of your people."

"What do you mean?"

He pulled one of the water-purification tablets from the pouch and twirled it between his fingers. "Is this what happened to your tribe? Were you defeated and had to survive by gifts?"

Nina noted his tone was innocent, not bitterly rhetorical. He genuinely wanted to know. Even so, his question puzzled her. "I don't understand."

"Where did this come from?" he said, bringing the pill close to his eye, still talking. "Do you even know? Before all this," he said, waving toward the cave and the mining operation, "I knew where everything I ate and everything I used came from. It came from the jungle and I knew how it was made. But now, I am ignorant. I am dependent. Somewhere far away are people being murdered to make this tablet? Do your people even ask these questions?"

"We try to live as best we can. None of us are perfect."

"But why do your people need our gift from the gods? Don't they have their own?"

"They don't need it. They just want it."

"How much do they want?"

"I don't know. I can't explain all of my people any more than you can explain every one of yours. Could you explain your father?"

Ndiko's gaze whipped at her with the force of a slap. She stepped back, her heart racing. A tense moment passed until he looked away from her.

"Is there an end to your tribe's want?" he said. "How wretched an existence, to forever be wanting, to never be satisfied, like hunger pains that never leave no matter how much you eat."

Nina cut him off. "Is there anything else you would like me to get for you?"

"I should be going. This will help, thank you," he said, stepping backwards. "Be careful." He charged into the thick jungle and disappeared.

Nina stood alone, her hands shaking.

7

The doorbell rang.

"Billy! Can you answer that? I'm busy," Teri yelled from her bedroom.

"All right." Billy paused his video game and stomped down the steps. Without looking outside, he yanked open the front door.

"Joe!" he yelled.

"And you thought I wouldn't show," Joe said.

"Well, kind of."

"It's all right. I'm here."

"I saw you in the papers. You were talking about the Huapi."

"Let's not worry about that, okay, Ace? Tonight let's just hang out like old times. Nothing but movies and fun."

* * *

The movie was an hour in when Joe stopped it. The TV switched to its default channel, showing an infomercial for a buttocks-flattening appliance.

"I'm going to get another drink," he said, "Anyone want anything?" he looked to Teri first. She yawned and nodded her head no. He looked to Billy. The boy was sleeping quietly next to her.

"He's out," Teri said.

"Already?"

"The new meds are much more powerful," Teri said, patting her son's hand. "They take a toll." The boy shifted and mumbled, but didn't wake up.

"Poor kid."

Teri raised the remote control as the TV silently displayed the colorful graphics of a news segment on Crystal Clay and Christmas.

"I'll change the channel," she said.

"No. Leave it."

"I don't think it's-"

"Quiet!"

He snatched the remote from her and turned up the volume, squatting in front of the TV.

A reporter laughed as he stood beside a group of children. A MajorCo Toys store's glowing sign gleamed in the sky over his shoulder, framed perfectly by the camera operator.

"I'm outside a local toy store, interviewing some experts on what kids want this holiday season. So, are you all ready for Christmas?" the reporter asked, leaning down, holding his microphone out.

"Yeah!" the children squealed.

"What do you want?"

"Crystal Clay!" the first one shouted.

"Oh, really? I've heard of that. It's the plastic thing that shows a rainbow in the light, and even in the dark, right?"

"Yeah!"

"That seems to be a popular toy this year," he smiled into the camera. "Any particular shape you want?"

"All of them!"

"All of them? Do you think Santa can swing that for you?"

"He sure can!"

"All right. I guess you've been good. Now, on to the next one," he shuffled over to the next child. "What do you want for Christmas?"

"Crystal Clay!"

"And why is that?"

"Colors. I like the colors. And the shapes. They're cool."

"Cool, huh? Well, you can't get a better endorsement than that. And what about you, little miss?"

"Crystal Clay."

"There seems to be a theme here. And you?"

"Crystal Clay!"

"You?"

"Crystal Clay!"

"Well, it's unanimous," he said, shrugging at the camera. "I just have one question. Why do they call it clay if you can't shape it into anything?"

The children stared at him, silent. One finally raised his hand. "Crystal Clay is fun!" he said .

"Well, there you have it, folks. If you didn't know what to get for the little ones in your life at Christmas this year, now you know."

Joe clicked off the TV and flopped onto the couch, rubbing his neck. "Who am I kidding? I can't stop it," he said, his shoulders sagging. "I can't. No one can."

"It's okay," Teri said, putting her arm around him. "You didn't know. Did you want all this to happen? No. What did you do? You saved a man's life. And you made my son smile."

He didn't respond.

Teri grabbed his chin and turned his face toward her. "Are you listening to me?"

"I'm just, so angry." He snapped away from her, leapt up and began pacing. "How am I going to stop this? It's not going to end. People don't just un-want something."

"Joe, calm down. Billy's sleeping."

"Calm down? People's lives are being shredded. And they're blaming me. People have died. Don't you get that?"

"Not because of you, Joe. If you had to do it again, would you let the chief die?"

"That's the past. It can't be changed. What am I going to do?"

"You can't stop it," a voice said from nearby. Joe froze. Billy, barely awake, pushed himself to a sitting position.

"You can't stop it," he said. "You just have to learn to live with it. Accept it. That's what I do with my cancer."

"Billy," Teri began.

"It's true, Mom. It's the best I can do. I just don't get upset about it. The doctor said bad things happen sometimes and all we can do is move forward, live with it."

"Honey, don't talk like that," Teri said. "We're sorry we woke you up. Please, go back to sleep."

"All right, but can you both be quiet?"

"I'm sorry, Billy," Joe said.

"It's okay," the boy yawned and leaned back, closing his eyes again.

Teri glared at Joe. "I think you'd better leave."

"I'm sorry," he said, "I can-"

"Please," she whispered. "Just go."

Part 9

1

Ndiko shuffled through the smog around him. Still suffering from insomnia, he had taken to walking in circles around the village, enacting a weak patrol. His upper back hurt from sagging. He no longer stood proud and defiant, but instead slouched as he walked, withered and tired.

Deep into the jungle where his sight was obscured by pollution, he heard faint young voices singing. He followed the sound until he saw shapes that appeared to be a man, a woman and three children following along.

Ndiko kept his distance, tracking them. He couldn't make out their faces, but judging by their singing, they were definitely Huapi.

The children started to sing again. The woman spun around and hissed until they quieted.

Ndiko followed. They were moving quickly, carrying nothing, heading away from the village toward the edge of Palagua City. They were cutting a wide path away from the mine, avoiding the guards.

When they were far beyond Huapi land, but not quite to the city, Ndiko raced to overtake them.

Still hiding in the foliage, he yelled out.

"Where are you going?"

The man and woman froze. The children yelped and cried. After some whispered scolding from the woman, they quieted.

"What are you afraid of?" Ndiko asked, emerging from the brush. "Where are you going?"

The man trotted back to face Ndiko. His eyes flew open in terror on seeing who had followed them.

"Ndiko," Waho whispered.

"Waho. My friend. Where are you going?"

His friend spoke with his head bowed, avoiding eye contact. "Look around, Ndiko. Our air stinks. Our land is being broken apart and stolen. Our people have been killed and we are all sick. I don't believe the pales are ever going to leave."

Ndiko nodded, frowning, and didn't argue.

"Our water is poison," Waho continued. "Those tablets you get from the pale lady, what are they? What evil magic might they hold? Where do they come from?"

Ndiko ignored his friend's increasingly hysterical tone. "Where are you all going? Where are you taking your family? Please be honest with me."

"I've been talking to someone."

"Talking to someone?"

"Someone not in our tribe."

Ndiko accepted this. If Nina was smuggling supplies to him, surely others could meet people from the outside. "Why did you keep it a secret from me?"

"I thought you would be angry."

"I'm not angry."

"You're lying, my Chief."

"I am more sad than angry. Please, just talk to me."

Waho looked past Ndiko, his eyes vacant and blissful as he spoke. "They told me that there is a life after this one, a time of peace and happiness, where there is no sickness, no death, no fear, no stealing of the land, no killing of our friends. There is only justice and peace."

"And this is for everyone? A gift from the pales? Like the tablets?"

"The only price is that I must swear mine and my family's loyalty forever to The Great Chief Lardesus."

"Lard Hesus? The pale god?"

"Lardesus!" the children cheered and the woman echoed with reverence.

Waho smiled vacantly, his eyes focusing in space somewhere above as he spoke.

"Lardesus will save us. You should join us, Ndiko. Lardesus will save you too. The time of the Huapi is over. They told me that the pales have always killed for what they want, they have always taken everything they want, and they have never lost a war. All because of Lardesus."

"They told you this? And it gave you hope?"

"Yes! We dare not defy Lardesus. Your father-"

"My father." Ndiko hung his head.

"When we were boys, your father talked of how huge our land was. Now it is but a parcel against the mountains. Almost nothing. I was not filled with hope when your father told me his stories. His tales were always the same: the pales take everything, they murder everyone, and they never lose anything in return. The Huapi are fewer, their land gets smaller. Your father's stories filled me with fear. But when the pales told me of Lardesus, I thought of what could be. They always win, Ndiko. Because of their great god."

"The pales lie, Waho."

"I know that. You always think I am stupid. Why? Because I was afraid when we attacked the pales? But I don't care what you think of me anymore. When they kill you, there will be nothing more. But when I die, Lardesus will grant me eternal life."

"Waho. My friend. You have lived in this jungle for as long as I have. You know that life comes and goes. The dead feed another round of life. There is no eternal life. There is only the cycle. We never had need of Lardesus before. Why now?"

"I knew you wouldn't understand. That's why I tried to sneak out."

Ndiko sighed. "You cannot answer my question."

"Why now? Because the end is near. Isn't it enough to know you'll all be killed? You cannot stop them. Our land is what they want. Either we join them or be destroyed."

"Seems to me you are both."

The blissful look left Waho's eyes, replaced by a cold stare.

"Come," he said to his family, "we are leaving."

"Lardesus!" the children cheered. They began walking.

Ndiko grabbed Waho's arm roughly. "When Lardesus betrays your family, when you are all slaves to the pales, I hope you burn with guilt for what you've done to your children."

"This," Waho said, snapping his arm free, "this anger of yours is part of the reason we're leaving. You've solved nothing. You are no chief. You are all going to die."

"We will die as Huapi. You will die as a coward and a slave." Ndiko turned away and did not look back.

2

The television:

News headlines scrolled across the bottom of the screen as the gel-haired newsreader read his prompter. People wearing suits walked among rows of screens behind him.

"Welcome to *The Business Report Comment Hour*, discussing everything happening in the marketplace. Today on our show we'll be debating the new toy, Crystal Clay. I'm sure you've heard of this popular gift item that every child wants. Now, what could possibly be so controversial about a toy? Just ask Joe Vera, the man who discovered the mineral Crystal Clay is made from. Last week he held a press conference to explain why he was turning against the product, but MajorCo Toys stock continues to soar. A trend this hot can't be pushed away that easily. Are Vera's comments just noise in the wind? Or are they part of a building storm? We're taking your calls. Caller, go ahead."

"Thanks for taking my call. Our American consumer dollars can help. The Palaguan people have never known this much wealth. I think we should all just keep buying Crystal Clay to help out their fledgling democracy. American dollars are a gift to American workers and the Palaguan economy."

"But caller, what do you make about the information Mister Vera presented in his news conference? That the mine for Crystal Clay, in Palagua, is sitting directly on the sacred land of the Huapi, a native tribe?"

"I'm sure if something illegal was being done, someone would sue."

"All right, thank you, caller. Next. Go ahead."

"Am I on?"

"Yes. Please state your point."

"Is this the call-in TV show?"

"Yes. Your point, caller?"

"I just want to say, I am sick and tired of everyone turning everything into a problem. It's like they don't want anyone to have any fun. They're all just a bunch of damn hippies. And this Vera character? I wish I had his money so I could complain about it like he does. I'm going to buy Crystal Clay for my grandkids and they're going to love it! It's my right."

"All right. Thank you. Next."

"Hello? Am I on? Oh. Good. I just wanted to say that business is business and if those Hoopees down there, or whatever they're called, don't like it, they can just move somewhere else. People should stop trying to halt progress. There's no stopping demand. If they only had some economics education, they would know that."

"Thank you caller. Next."

"Hello? I can't believe you're a business show hosting this debate. I'm putting everything I own into MajorCo Toys stock. I've already made a bundle, and I'm going all in now. Crystal Clay all the way, baby!"

"Thank you, caller! Well, it's not much of a debate so far. Just some ringing endorsements for Crystal Clay. If there's anyone on the other side of this issue out there, please feel free to call in."

3

Ndiko sat on the ground and watched the sun rise as Waho's words set fire to his blood. Morning came and the village trudged about its business. The Huapi moved among the smog, bent, coughing and holding their bellies. The noise of the machines nearby discouraged most talking.

The men prepared wearily for their hunt. "Ndiko? Are you okay?" they asked him. He didn't respond. They shook him, smacked his head, but he didn't move. He simply kept staring. After several futile efforts to get him to acknowledge them, they shrugged and left.

When they returned a couple hours later, Ndiko had not moved.

The women crept by him as they prepared to gather fruits, their eyes fearful. He didn't move. The earth shook under him, driving the roots and rocks he was resting on further into his back. Those women who stayed behind to watch the children kept glancing his way while they tended to their duties.

He ate nothing, he drank nothing. His mother tried to make him respond by talking to him, but then she too gave up and left him alone in his trance. The noise from the mine continued all day, the stench intensifying until it finally faded with the setting sun.

The rest of the tribe noticed Ndiko was in the same place and position they had left him in the morning. He blinked, but stared straight ahead at nothing.

They whispered as they prepared their food, dropping the tablets Nina had brought into bowls of boiling water.

As the sun set, Ndiko rose. All eyes of the village turned to him.

"We will do something," he told the men huddled around the cooking fire.

"Tonight."

* * *

The Palaguan security guard staggered deeper into the jungle, laughing hysterically. He and his fellow watchmen on night shift were stoned on the chewy bark from the jungle trees.

As he sought a good spot to piss, he thought to himself how lucky he was to have this job. The Americans had taken an interest in Palagua, and the jobs at the mine paid well. The job also gave him a convenient excuse to avoid soldiering. The new government of the Palaguan Revolutionary Movement left him alone, and he was able to excuse himself from the guerilla recruiters for the deposed government, its survivors now planning a counter-rebellion.

On top of all those benefits, this was by far the easiest job he ever had. He simply walked among the machines and made sure no one came close to them. The most he had done was yell at gathering Huapi women who strayed too close to the mining road. He had seen no more of the savages since then.

The guard dropped his pants to relieve himself and yelled back at the others. They erupted in laughter and taunts. He stared up through the jungle roof and into the star-flecked sky.

Urinating while trying to retain his balance was proving difficult. He laughed as he staggered about.

There was suddenly a sharp pain in his abdomen, then another in his neck. He kept watching the stars, ignoring the pain, which was increasingly distant. He felt himself stumbling and falling. His head seemed to smack hard on a tree root, but he barely felt it. Suddenly he was looking down at his pants around his ankles. He tried to reach for them but and he couldn't move.

Laughing was suddenly an effort. He couldn't breathe. Then he noticed the pain in his abdomen came from a small arrow. Men were staring down at him. They weren't Palaguan. They weren't American. They had to be the Huapi.

He tried to scream and reach for his gun, but he was paralyzed. The bark's juice was blazing through his veins, mixing with the poison from the dart tip.

The Huapi lifted him, and it was a delightful, enjoyable feeling until they set him down and attacked him with crude knives.

* * *

What began as another day at the mine turned into chaos. The miners had been filing into the caves, but suddenly they were turning around, running back the way they had come, some vomiting as they stumbled into the light.

The guards clung together and readied their guns. They moved forward slowly, coming across the night guard's skinned body hung from a tree.

"Cut him down and get everyone back to work!" the Palaguan foreman shouted to his guards.

Then he ducked into the woods to throw up.

4

"Oh, hi. It's you."

Billy tried to appear disappointed as he yanked open his home's front door, but Joe could tell the boy was pleased to see him.

"Hey, Ace. What's going on? How do you like the care center? Your mom told me you had good things to say about it."

"The new place is okay. The doctors and nurses are much nicer than the stupid hospital. It's fun, but I still hate the meds."

"Everyone hates the meds, but you have to do them. Can I come in?"

"I guess," Billy let his hand drop from the doorknob, heading back into the house, hanging his shoulders in mock apathy.

Kid, don't ever be an actor, Joe thought to himself.

Teri entered the room. "Billy, who was that? Oh! Joe," she said, surprised.

"I'm here."

"Great! Billy, isn't this great? Joe's here."

Her son flopped himself on the couch and let his head roll back, staring at the ceiling.

"Yeah. Maybe."

"Come on," Joe pleaded, "I know I've been busy lately and I haven't been around, but I always think of you."

"You haven't called in over a week," Billy said, still not looking at him. "You never stop by anymore."

Teri folded her arms and shrugged, raising her eyebrows at Joe.

"He's got a good point."

"Fair enough," Joe said. "I've been working hard to put an end to Crystal Clay."

"I heard about you on the news a couple of times," Billy said, "but all the kids at school and the clinic are crazy for it. Whatever you're doing, it's not working."

Joe sighed. "I know. But I'm trying."

"Me too," Billy said. "I tell the other kids it's bad for the Huapi people, that it's like stealing, but they just look at me weird or run away."

"That's good, though," Joe said. "You have to try."

"Like you try to visit us?" Billy asked, still staring at the ceiling.

Joe looked to Teri for help but found none.

"I'm trying now, Billy. I came by to schedule a date. This Friday. Yes, I've been busy, but that's no excuse for neglecting my friends. So I'm setting aside time. Do we have a deal?"

Billy lifted his head and finally made eye contact. "Promise?"

Joe paused and looked at Teri. She offered him a lopsided grin, but nothing else.

"I will be here," Joe said.

"You didn't promise," Billy said, looking back up at the ceiling, sighing.

"Okay, I promise. I will be here Friday. I promise."

"We'll see then," Billy said, and clicked the television on with the remote.

* * *

When Billy fell asleep, Joe and Teri left the room.

"Here," Joe whispered as he handed Teri a check. "I need to give it to you now."

"Joe, I don't want your money."

"You have to take it. If you don't, they'll take it from me. If I give it to you, they can't get it. Cash it immediately. I signed an agreement that I wouldn't say anything negative about MajorCo Toys. But I'm their worst nightmare now. It's probably only a matter of time before they sue me. So take it. Once it's yours, they can't legally touch it. At least, I don't think they can. If they try, hire a lawyer."

"Joe, this is how much I make in a year." She steadied herself against a bookcase.

"Now you can take a year off." He smiled weakly.

"Thank you," she hugged him and kissed him on the cheek.

"I just hope I can stop this mess I've caused."

"Well, to me, it's not a mess. It's a blessing."

"Don't remind me."

"Of course I feel sorry for the people in Palagua, but, well, I need money. Billy needs money. And treatment. You have a good heart, Joe."

"Let's not talk about it. Let's just not think about it."

"You're right," she said, folding the check neatly and slipping it in her pocket. "That's probably best."

5

The television:

Three men sat on a stage, Joe Vera on the left, Ethan Scherr on the right, the host in the middle.

The host leaned out of his chair at such an angle he was practically squatting. He spoke with hyperactive, red-faced excitement.

"Today on *Debate Gladiators!* One's a rising executive at corporation behind the hottest stock on the market. The other is an outsider, challenging his former company. They used to be partners! Now they're on opposite sides! What happened to turn these former friends into vicious enemies? Mister Vera, I'll start with you! You've made millions just by telling MajorCo Toys where you had obtained the raw material for the white-hot seller Crystal Clay. Why are you now turning against them?"

Joe made sure he didn't look at Ethan. "I've never regretted a decision more in my life," he said. "The MajorCo Toys Corporation is making Crystal Clay by decimating the native people's sacred land. The natural resources, the water, the forest, all that they count on for their survival is being polluted. The area is becoming unlivable. If I could give all my money back and have this never have happened, I would. Unfortunately, there's no way to bring the murdered Huapi children back to life."

"I need to interject," Scherr said.

"It's your turn anyway," the host turned, flinging sweat across the stage.

"There were several inaccuracies in what Mister Vera just stated," Scherr said. "The MajorCo Toys Corporation has never, ever condoned murder. Nor is it being carried out."

"No one is saying they condoned it," Joe said, "but you are carrying it out. Killing their land kills them."

"Just a minute!" the host said, flailing at Joe. "Mister Scherr is permitted his time for rebuttal."

"I just wanted to say," Scherr continued, "that MajorCo Toys has never ever condoned or endorsed the killing of anyone. To suggest otherwise is utterly ridiculous. This is a toy. To make the toy, we mine a natural resource that the government of Palagua has agreed to sell to us. There is nothing at all illegal about this."

The host leaned back and emitted fake laughter, his face turning a deep red. "Now, come on, guys, are you sure this isn't some publicity stunt to get people talking even more about MajorCo's new product Crystal Clay? The old 'any news is good news' approach?"

"Absolutely not," Joe said. "I am no longer affiliated with MajorCo Toys, since Huapi were murdered during the mining process."

"That's not true!" Ethan yelled.

"But there were some Huapi killed, weren't there?" the host asked.

"Killed is not murdered. There was a misunderstanding."

The host chuckled. "That must have been some misunderstanding."

"The Huapi have occupied that land for centuries," Joe said. "It's how they live. Then, suddenly, some miners show up and start shooting them."

Shifting in his seat, the host addressed Joe. "Look. Let's get specific. Exactly how many Huapi are we talking here?"

Ethan answered for him. "Three, by all reliable accounts. Some miners were also killed. By the Huapi."

"One miner," Joe said. "The Huapi counter-attacked because their land was being destroyed and the forest that sustains them. Americans should know that the toys they buy are killing people."

The host interrupted. "Toys killing people? I mean, I don't want to put a value on lives, but we're only talking four people here, right? Four people is bad of course, but it isn't exactly a genocide. Accidents do happen."

"And that's just what this was," Ethan said. "An extremely unfortunate incident. That's all."

"The Huapi are a tribe consisting of only about one hundred people. Every loss is felt immensely," Joe said.

"All right," the host said. "Now this is making me think I should grab my children's Crystal Clay toys and return them, despite the tears. Any thoughts, Mister Scherr?"

"I think what's being overlooked here is the major benefits to the Palaguan people. Do you know how many Palaguans died because of a poor urban infrastructure? With American dollars pouring in, Palagua is suddenly an emerging market on the world stage. The whole society can suddenly implement advances in food preservation, healthcare and other improvements we here in the States take for granted."

"What about the Huapi?!" Joe shouted.

"What about the rights of Americans?" Scherr screamed, his voice shrill.

"Rights of Americans? Right to destroy the Huapi and their way of life? What should I do, Ethan? Shoot someone to make them stop?"

"Shoot someone? You mean consumers? Shoot the American consumer?" the host asked. "Is that a threat?"

"No, I'm wondering what will make the point," Joe said. "I want to know, from Ethan, how would he like me to protest this? I'm being peaceful. What could I say or do that would be acceptable to you? Nothing. I disagree and I want people to stop buying. Isn't it my right to say that?"

Scherr turned to the host. "Listen to him. He wants to shout me down, infringing on my right to speak. He wants to shoot people. He is against the right of the American people to purchase what they want and he is against the right of the Palaguan people to sell what they want. He essentially says 'Your way of life needs to end.' He uses the language of terrorists."

Somewhere deep inside, Joe felt something break as his temper became unglued.

"Terrorists?" Joe boomed. "You're calling me a terrorist when your company is indirectly responsible for those killed? All for a toy?"

"I didn't kill anyone," Ethan said.

"You sure as hell facilitated it."

"So now you're calling the average American a terrorist, just for buying a toy?"

"I'm saying you're a bastard who doesn't care about anything but money!"

Joe leapt from his chair and swung at Ethan. Ethan ducked then leapt up. They squared off, swinging and pushing. Stagehands rushed in from all angles and pulled the two apart.

The host smiled broadly.

"Fantastic! Did you get that?" he asked the camera crew. "You did? Good. Now get these two idiots out of here."

* * *

Later that night, in the MajorCo Toys marketing meeting room, Scherr paced to shake off his agitation. The marketing team watched the video clip of *Debate Gladiators*, ending with him and Joe Vera throwing punches as they were swarmed by black-shirted stagehands.

The CEO frowned at him. "You did well, Scherr, but I shouldn't have to say we would prefer to avoid this kind of theater."

Ethan nodded agreement. "I understand. That part's my fault. I simply felt we couldn't let his story go unchallenged."

"Understandable. And it's perfectly acceptable that you went. Once. From now on, no more confrontation. Just let this go. Let Vera do his thing and we'll just carry on as if we're innocent."

Someone in the room coughed politely.

"I meant because we're innocent."

* * *

Joe's press agent screamed at him. "What the hell were you thinking taking a swing at him? You look like an idiot now. A thug. You're hurting your own cause."

"I don't care, I'm sick of this debate. People are dying and Ethan and MajorCo and every person in the world is talking as if I'm violating some human right just by asking them not to buy a stupid toy."

"Joe, would you listen to yourself? We're the ones who specialize in public relations. Not you. You sound nuts. This didn't help your cause at all. You have to be patient. And classy. You're the underdog here."

"I don't care. I'm sick of waiting. I need to do this hands-on. Maybe I'll chain myself to something."

"Now, Joe. Come on. That can sometimes work. But I have to tell you stunts are very unpredictable. They are as likely to turn opinion against you. You need to give it time."

"The Huapi don't have time."

He stormed out of the office, slamming the door behind him.

6

Nina took every step with care, crouching low as she moved. Her lower back ached, her calves burned. She dared not stand up. She had never seen so many guards along the mining road, all running back and forth, calling out to each other. Something terrible must have happened recently to trigger such an increase in security.

She smelled the village before she saw it. Flies clouded her path, slowing her progress, as she was forced to flail her arms constantly or be stung. The heat, the stench of feces and smog, the relentless rumble of trucks and power equipment combined to test her resolve.

Her package of supplies tumbled as she tripped over a root. She fell to her knees and fumbled for her backpack. Flies stung her arms, face, and exposed legs.

She sobbed in frustration, slapping at her wounded skin.

"Come on, girl," she said. "Get a hold of yourself."

She wiped her nose and proceeded onward, crawling, when she heard shouting coming from the village.

From a distance, she could see Huapi shoving each other, cursing, arguing. She crawled closer, listening.

"I thought you might come this way," a nearby voice said.

Nina yelped, surprised. She looked back and saw Yuala leaning against a tree, looking at the ground, her head sagging to one side with a combination of exhaustion and sadness.

"Yuala," Nina said. "What's going on?"

"Oh. They're arguing." She absently plucked a flower from a nearby vine and then tossed it back into the forest.

"Are you hurt?"

"No."

"You don't seem well."

"I'm not."

"Should I-"

"Some think we should leave. Some think we should fight. Some think we should move. I think we should allow our life to run its course. Either our time has ended and our land will be destroyed or the pales will leave. There is no need to let the struggle against the end corrupt us."

Ndiko crashed through the brush and stood before them. He was panting, his eyes bulging, his face flushed. The yelling back in the village center continued.

"Mother," Ndiko scolded, "I told you not to leave my side. Ever!"

Yuala nodded meekly, her eyes glazed in total resignation.

"Ndiko," Nina said, "what happened?"

He turned, finally noticing her, and raised his spear. "I should kill you," he said, "You're nothing but a pale. Just like the other."

Nina stepped back, "What do you mean, just like the other?"

Ndiko smiled evilly. "You don't know about the pale we killed yesterday?"

"Leave," Yuala said to Nina.

"What other?" Nina said. "What happened?"

"Leave!" Yuala muttered. "Never come back."

Ndiko chuckled. "Then why do you stay, mother?"

"Because I love a son I no longer know," she whispered.

"You killed another miner?" Nina asked.

"We did," Ndiko said. "We tortured him and strung up his corpse."

"My son," Yuala whispered as she stared at the ground.

"You idiot!" Nina screamed. "They will come back for you. They will avenge as you avenged. Didn't you learn anything?"

"Run, girl!" Yuala cried. "Run and leave us here to die!"

Ndiko laughed and twirled his spear. "Yes, please. Leave."

Nina turned to run, then stopped in her tracks. The armed guards from the mine were marching quickly from the road toward the village, shoulder to shoulder.

"Oh, no," Nina said.

The line pushed through the foliage, passing by quickly. She, Ndiko and Yuala stared as they might watch a passing parade.

Nina dropped to the ground and covered her head with her arms. The passing men had reached the edge of the village. They raised their weapons and fired. Smoke and screams filled the air. Huapi people ran everywhere. The line of security guards fired another volley, sweeping forward.

Ndiko vanished into the jungle, yelling, his spear flying into the line, cutting down a man.

Nina stayed low, screaming away the noise as gunshots continued to ring out. Spears whistled through the green. There were shouts of position, cries for help in Huapi and Palaguan. Bullets thunked into tree trunks all around her. Footsteps thundered in all directions.

It was a slaughter, a war. Nina looked up to try to find a way out, but couldn't make out anything through the smoke.

She lay still, praying until the sounds retreated.

Yuala was still leaning against a tree, eyes wide.

Nina slithered to her.

"Yuala, get down. Lie down. It's not safe."

Yuala's head was resting against the tree as when Nina had found her earlier. Her eyes stared, unseeing. Nina shook her but the older woman didn't move. Her head fell forward, limp, a neat black hole from a bullet in her temple.

Nina gasped, and stretched Yuala' body on the ground.

"I'm sorry," Nina said.

She then leapt up and ran.

7

The MajorCo Toys store front was nearly obscured by the many strands of Christmas garland and colored lights.

A weak winter sun rose over the full parking lot, barely shining through the sky's overcast.

Determined parents stood in the cold, breathing steam, fondling their credit cards. Less-determined parents waited in their cars, the engine running and heater on while talking on their phones, listening to the radio or tapping the steering wheel.

Fluorescent lights flickered on inside the store, adding to the anticipation. The soft sound of snow crunching underfoot grew louder as the pacing of those waiting outside quickened.

Within the glass entrance lobby, the manager, clearly identifiable by his gold nametag and pale collared shirt, approached the front doors. The shoppers moved in close, much like fish swimming quickly to the surface of an aquarium when a feeding hand approaches.

The manager checked his watch, shook his head and turned away from the doors. "Five more minutes," he yelled through the glass to the waiting shoppers. He held his hand up, fingers spread out.

"What are you here to get?" one waiting parent asked another.

"Crystal Clay," the other answered.

"Who isn't here to get Crystal Clay?" a third asked. They all chuckled lightly.

"Hey, watch it!" a voice yelled from the back of the crowd.

Someone was shoving their way through to the front.

"End of the line!"

He was a tall man in a large trench coat, a knit cap pulled down almost over his eyes. He clinked as he walked, as if he had lots of change in his pocket.

"Hey, jerk, the manager said he was going to open the store in five minutes! Get in line like the rest of us."

The man crashed against the doors, his jacket billowing out. Some waiting shoppers laughed.

"Is he drunk?"

"The guy said five minutes!" someone repeated.

Joe rubbed his head against the door to pry off his cap.

"The store's closed," he said over his shoulder.

"We know that," someone else replied.

"Closed all day," Joe said.

He stepped back as far he could and showed the shoppers the chain around his wrists and waist that he had threaded through the handles of the front door.

"Oh, man, you've got to be kidding me," one of the shoppers said.

Joe screamed as loud as he could. "This is for the Huapi! Boycott Crystal Clay! You're driving them off their land! You're killing them! Save the Huapi!"

"You're doing this for who?" someone asked, but the question was lost in screaming. The shoppers shoved Joe against the door, reached around him, trying to pull him free. He let them try.

From the other side of the door, the store manager fiddled with his keys to find the right one.

"Store's closed!" Joe yelled to him. The manager looked up. Joe nodded toward the chain running through the door handles.

The manager cursed and turned away, whipping out his cell phone.

Joe pressed himself against the door and closed his eyes. He ignored the screams and the kicks and punches landing on his back. He relished the sound of parents cursing as they retreated to their cars, engines fading into the distance to begin the hunt for Crystal Clay elsewhere.

"For the Huapi!" Joe yelled, over and over again until he was hoarse.

8

"Hey!" someone called.

Nina glanced back to see who was chasing her. The guards from the mine were crashing toward her through the jungle.

"Hey! Get over here! It's not safe! You're not supposed to be here!"

Nina bounded on. She was running for her life now, running panicked. She had no idea where she was going. She couldn't see through the gun smoke and smog more than several paces in front of her.

The voice calling to her drifted away.

She forced herself to keep going, even as she was gasping for air, her breaths ragged. If she stopped, she would not be able to move again for a long time. She put her sorrow for Yuala far away in her heart. Yuala was gone and she would be too if she didn't keep going. Keep on moving, she thought, this is for your life.

She had to tell someone, had to let the outside world know. The mining company was killing the Huapi. Slaughtering them.

"Screw it," she said, and changed her direction. She headed toward the mine, trudging through foliage, sobbing and sniffing as she went. She was in a world of her own, a tiny space of clarity moving through a smog-shrouded forest, walking on forever in the crushing heat, enduring a solitary damnation.

Finally, the large orange slab of a truck's flank emerged from the grey. It was backed to the edge of the area where Crystal Clay was brought up by hand from the mine.

She inspected the vehicle from the edge of the forest, selecting her target carefully, gathering her breath.

A man stood in the back of the truck, kicking crates of raw crystal so they could be stacked to capacity. The driver leaned against the other side of the truck and smoked.

Nina stomped across the open area and pulled open a panel on the side of the truck, reached in and yanked out wires. She lifted a rock from the ground and began pummeling the circuitry. It dissolved before her with satisfying cracking sounds.

The man in the truck-bed yelled. The driver came around the front and snatched at her. She hit him in the head with the rock. He staggered back and then rushed at her, grabbing her around the waist. She bit his ear until he let go. Blood dribbled down her chin. The driver held his ear and cursed.

She pushed him aside and sprinted away.

Part 10

1

A phone rang in the offices of the new Palaguan government. The recently-appointed Minister of Palaguan Business Affairs picked it up.

"The guard has been avenged," the caller said.

"His family will be pleased."

"They would be doubly pleased if they could see."

"Enough. I don't need to know more. The money we gave them has also played a part in calming their weeping hearts."

"The Americans will now see we are capable of handling problems quickly."

"Possibly."

"Possibly?"

"They now want more."

"More? More from the mine? Or, more, um, more actions like the one today?"

"Let me say they are willing to pay."

"Then we are willing to provide."

"Of course."

2

Joe couldn't stop his gasping, hysterical laughing.

He sounded insane. He felt insane. But they were letting him go from jail, and that, he thought, was very funny. The guards squinted at him as he climbed into the back of the cab.

The ride home was also hilarious. His driver sped off before Joe could close the door. Down the gravel driveway the door flapped loosely until the cab driver slammed on his brakes, momentum clicking the door shut. That was funny, too.

Joe staggered toward his mansion, bent-over laughing, tears streaming down his cheeks. He opened the door on his own car for something, then forgot what it was. He left the door open and continued up the porch stairs as the vehicle beeped a warning. He crashed inside his new home like a drunk, flopping down before the television.

He held the remote in his palm calmly, his laughter dying down. He clicked on the news.

The news was on.

"...and Joe Vera, the one-time beneficiary of MajorCo Toys' Crystal Clay, now its arch-enemy, staged a one-man protest today, chaining himself to the only entrance of one of MajorCo Toys' flagship stores."

"You idiots!" Joe yelled, his voice echoing inside his cavernous home. He felt shivering cold, then sweating hot, then back again and back again.

The phone rang.

"Yes, Teri. I know I shouldn't have," he chuckled as he lifted the receiver.

"My God my God my God my God my God! Oh, my God."

Joe laughed. "You definitely have the wrong number."

"Joe?" the voice said.

"Yes," he giggled.

"They killed them."

Joe laughed again.

"Joe Vera?"

"Yes."

"It's Nina. Nina Vasquez. They killed more Huapi. The Palaguan government raided the village to make way for the miners. Are you hearing me? There's more Huapi dead! I don't know how many. Maybe all of them. I think the soldiers saw me."

Joe chuckled again, feeling his sanity come loose.

"Are you... laughing?"

"No," Joe snorted.

"Damn it, Joe! What are we going to do? I had to tell someone. You're the only one who can help now. They're coming for me. Joe, you have to do something! Help!"

"I already did," he said, laughing. "I did all one man could do."

"Get it together, Joe. You've got to do more! Don't give up. "

"I chained myself to a toy store." Joe snickered like an irreverent schoolboy.

"You did what?" Nina screeched. Before he could answer, she whispered, "Someone's at my door!"

She hung up.

Joe threw the phone aside and slowly undressed.

"No one cares, Nina," he said, as he folded his clothing neatly. "Children, adults, mothers, fathers are killed, but who cares?"

He picked up a potted plant and hurled it at his television. Glass and dirt exploded into the room.

"Nobody cares! As long as they get what they want."

The dust from the atomized screen floated down in the sunlight.

He kicked off his shoes.

"I'm done!" he yelled.

He pulled his shirt over his head and threw it. It snagged on the chandelier and hung there.

"It's over."

He undid his belt, dropped his pants and flung them across the room. Now naked, he stretched his arms out to either side and spun around once. He breathed deeply and exhaled, satisfied, his eyes wild.

"From now on, I will know where it all comes from."

3

Teri hung up the phone after the twentieth ring, sighed, and turned to her son. Billy sat on the couch, resting his chin on his hand.

"He's not answering, honey," Teri said. "I'm sorry. Guess it's just you and me. Another Friday night date."

She spoke brightly, but she could feel the anger burning in her cheeks. The only thing keeping her rage in check was her indecision, should she be concerned or should she hope that something terrible had happened to Joe?

"I knew it," Billy said.

"I don't know if this will make you feel better, but he's making me angry, too."

"It doesn't matter. I'm going to die, anyway. He's probably just trying to get away from me early. And why not? The cancer is going to kill me, isn't it?"

Teri's jaw dropped, stunned. She stared deep into her son's eyes and was surprised at her response. "It might. Probably. Someday. We all die."

"I know that. But how soon?"

"Come on, kid. Don't think like that. We can't lose hope." A tear stole down her cheek. Billy wiped her face dry with his thumb. He smiled gently.

"Don't cry, Mom. I'll be all right. I'm just sick of lying and fakeness. I'm sick of Joe's empty promises. I don't have time for anything but the truth."

Teri burst into tears, hiding her face in her hands. Billy rested his hand on her shoulder. "I'll be okay, Mom. You've made me happy. I just wish-"

"I'm sorry..." she stammered.

"I wish I could grow up to be somebody," Billy said.

"You already are," she sniffed, reaching for a tissue and patting his head. "You're so brave."

"I'm not brave. All I'm doing is facing what I have to. And I just wish I had more time. I wish I could be stronger, healthier, all that."

She gasped again. "Any mother would be lucky to have a son like you. I love you just as you are now."

"Joe can go to hell," Billy growled.

Teri smirked through her tears. "You shouldn't say things like that, but right now, I agree."

4

The CEO of MajorCo Toys was smiling. From behind his podium, he looked out across the hotel ballroom. The vast hall glittered with Christmas decorations. Banners bearing the company logo crossed the ceiling. MajorCo Toys executives sipped champagne and talked excitedly. The CEO waved to the crowd and began his speech, his voice amplified across the cavernous room.

"This year was our best year ever! Our stock is higher than it's ever been. We had some hard times recently, and we had a lot of criticism. That's the price of success. The introduction of Crystal Clay into our product line was an enormous risk that paid off big. It wasn't without its struggles and setbacks. But one man weathered them all, a fearless captain on a fearsome sea. It gives me immense pleasure to announce MajorCo Toys' new employee of the year: Ethan Scherr!"

The ballroom exploded in applause and cheers. Ethan Scherr rose from his table and made his way to the stage slowly, weaving around the tables, shaking hands and exchanging hugs all the way to the front. He climbed the stairs to the stage and pumped his fist.

"Success!" he yelled into the crowd. "Success!" He held his fists above his head, forming a victory-V, like an athlete winning a championship. The CEO shook his hand, gave him a huge hug and whispered in his ear, "Great job, buddy. Great job."

5

The pounding on her door became increasingly violent. Nina ran to the back of her apartment. She pushed her body through her back window, spilling into an alley behind her home. She heard a crash as intruders smashed through her front door.

"Policía!"

Ignoring the scrapes on her hips, she scrambled to her feet and ran. The sun was setting, but the sky was dim light.

"Night, please hurry," she prayed.

She moved along the filthy back alleys, behind the homes where people threw their garbage and sometimes, when the Palagua City plumbing wasn't working, their own waste. She sprinted through the sludge, heading for the slums. The poorest section of town was the only place she could think to go. The people there would never cooperate with the police.

She found her way to a bar and entered. The place was so dark, it seemed night had already fallen. When her eyes adjusted, she ordered a drink and sat at a booth across from an unconscious drunk. His pants pockets were turned completely inside out. He snored loudly. No one cared.

She kept her head down over her drink and cried softly.

The man across from her stirred, and she almost vomited at the sight of vermin crawling around his scalp. She drank another sip from her mug and calmed herself.

Two hours to nightfall, then she would make her move.

The man across from her snorted loudly, shifted in his seat, and fell asleep again. She started to sob. No one paid them any attention.

* * *

Two agonizingly long hours passed. She paid with all the money she had to keep the drinks coming, and keep the bartender interested enough in her to glare at the other patrons when they eyed her with a predator's gaze. Even from behind the bar, the stocky, scarred man's gaze was enough to make them turn away.

Darkness finally came.

Nina made her way across the city, avoiding everyone she saw or heard. She suspected that the underpaid and corrupt police would not be looking for her at this hour, but she was taking no chances. If she saw movement or heard a sound, she went the other way.

The stars rose, and she jumped at every sound, running, hiding among the debris. She was completely lost, but fine with that. She nodded asleep leaning her back against an abandoned building.

She awoke with a small yelp and continued.

"Head for the forest," she said to herself. "The jungle."

Fear crept back into her at the same pace that orange crept back into the sky. Just as she began to worry that her cautious pace had been too slow, she saw the painted white crucifix above the mission. The mining road would be nearby, and beyond that, whatever was left of the Huapi.

If there were anyone left.

"Made it," she whispered.

Her hope was short-lived. From her hidden spot in the forest, she watched a group of about twenty Huapi, huddled together with their hands in the air, trudging down the mining road. They were surrounded by armed Palaguan guards.

Slowly the Huapi were formed into a single line. A man outside the mission blessed each of them as he or she walked by, pressing his palm against their forehead and speaking in Latin. Parents carried children and helped the elderly. Their gazes never rose; they stared at the ground clutching each other. They were ordered to remove their clothes and all jewelry, which they did.

Nina cried as she watched the entire naked mass of Huapi crowded together, surrounded by the miners' guns. The Huapi men shielded the women and children in the middle of their circle.

Hoses were turned on them. The water splintered off their naked backs and buttocks, knocking the children to the ground.

"Clean them, Lord! Clean them, Lord Jesus!" One missionary cried in English, as the Huapi were doused. After the spray stopped, each Huapi was then given a white robe to wear and made to sit in a circle.

"Where did this come from?" Nina whispered, offering a near-silent tribute to this chunk of the Huapi people, assimilated before her eyes. For all she knew they were the only survivors, the last remnant of the Huapi tribe.

The missionaries began a sermon in English. The Huapi huddled together and wept. A truck convoy rumbled down the road toward the mine, mercifully cutting the scene from Nina's sight.

* * *

She cut through the forest, toward the wreckage of the village.

"You're walking the wrong way," someone said. Startled, she jumped.

Ndiko was leaning against a tree, staring away from the village.

"Which way should I go?" she asked.

"Away. Into the forest. There is nothing left here. Nothing but death."

"I came to see what I could do."

Ndiko snorted. She continued, following the sounds of the wailing. He walked alongside her.

Every direction she looked, Huapi knelt on the ground, crying over their dead relatives.

"Where did this come from?" they cried. Some of them wailed, some whispered.

The corpses were neatly laid out in a row, ready to be dumped into the river. Yuala's body was turning a stiff purplish color. Ndiko gently stroked her hair. Nina did the same, offering a silent farewell prayer.

"What are you doing here?" Ndiko asked.

"I have nowhere to go."

"You are doomed if this is the only place you can be. Doomed like all of us."

"I thought there might still be hope."

"This place is the opposite of hope," Ndiko said. "We are destroyed. Look around." He turned to survey the smoldering remains of the village. Huapi were bleeding, shaking uncontrollably, clutching at their family helplessly as they died.

"We are finished," he said. "This is the end of the Huapi forever."

Part 11

1

"Dad! You're the best!"

Ethan Scherr smiled as his son Cory hugged him with all the strength a little boy could muster.

"Cory, let your father go," Ethan's wife said from the back seat of their minivan.

"He's all right, honey," Ethan said, "I can still drive."

"Happy Birthday, Cory!" the banner over the entrance to the amusement park read. They drove in and parked. A line of cars behind them pulled up nearby. Cory's entire class poured out, wildly racing for the rides.

"The whole park is ours?" the other children asked. "Cory, your dad is awesome!"

The parents let them go. The mothers hugged Ethan and the fathers shook his hand, slapped him on the back.

"Is that boy your ex-partner knows here? Billy Young?" Ethan Scherr's wife asked when the children had run off.

Ethan looked around. "Cory invited the whole class, like we told him to do, but Billy's not doing well. His health is failing. I doubt Joe will show. I really hope he doesn't, but I didn't want our issues to get in the way of the celebration. We couldn't exclude anybody. If he does show, he better not make a scene about the Crystal Clay party favors."

"You did the right thing, honey, and it worked out."

"Sure did," Ethan joked. "Good thing that kid has terminal cancer!"

His wife punched him in the arm. "Honey!"

Ethan smiled. "You know I don't mean it, but let's be honest, it makes things easier if he's not here."

2

Nina felt someone kicking her. She roused from sleep slowly. She was lying on the ground somewhere in the midst of the ruin that once was the Huapi village.

"You want to help?" Ndiko asked.

"What?" she said. Her head was pounding.

"You want to help? You always talk about wanting to help."

"Yes. Sure."

"Then help me care for my mother's body. We can take care of the others after."

Nina swallowed hard. They had stacked the corpses near the river last night, before she collapsed from exhaustion. While she had been asleep the surviving Huapi had covered each body with kindling and leaves to prepare it for burning before being given to the river.

She winced as she looked at the stiff, blue face of Yuala. The once cheerful smiling woman was still forever.

"Oh, Mother," Ndiko sighed, sounding more impatient than sorrowful, "at least you won't see the end of our people. Just like father did not."

Nina said nothing. She watched him as he stared at his mother's hardened face. "Gather more sticks," he finally said. "The body must be burned quickly, so it may return to the jungle as soon as possible. It is the way of setting things right."

She was grateful for something to do, something away from the corpses.

When enough wood had been gathered, Ndiko stood over the unlit pyre, a flaming torch raised above his head. Nina waited for him to say something, but he did not.

Silently, slowly, he lowered his arm to several spots around the pile. The bed of twig caught fire almost immediately. They stepped back and watched his mother's body burn.

In the distance, she could hear miners yelling back and forth to each other as another truck revved its engine and rumbled away toward the Palagua City docks.

Ndiko did not seem to hear. Tears streamed down his face but he made no sound. They stood there watching the fire, until Nina's legs hurt, and her lungs burned from breathing in the thickening smoke. She was determined not to step back, but she had to so she wouldn't pass out. After an eternity, the mound of sticks began to collapse.

"Now," Ndiko said. They lifted the two logs under the burning mat, sending the ashen remains of Yuala, still burning, into the river, to drift out to sea.

Ndiko turned away immediately. "Now the others."

They worked through the day and night, each body given the same reverential but hasty treatment and burial. Nina worked alongside the remaining Huapi; she estimated there were less than two dozen left.

They disappeared into the forest and returned at random intervals. She didn't ask their names. There was work to be done and no time for formalities as body after body was burned.

3

How long had it been?

Joe had no idea.

The sun rose and fell. The moon followed. Then the sun again, then the moon. He wasn't counting.

He simply went about living: food, water, shelter, warmth. The only measure of time was the fact that nearly all his furniture was gone. He had destroyed it to feed his nightly cooking fire, and to keep himself from freezing. The once-pristine white walls of his home were now covered with splotches of soot.

He took the last of his brand new, expensive, wooden chairs, hoisted it over his head and swung it against the floor. The chair exploded into several pieces. He gathered up the remnants and threw them into the bonfire in the center of his high-ceiling living room.

He sat down on his scuffed and blackened tile floor, scratching his beard vigorously. Not taking a shower for several days (or weeks?) had taken its toll on his skin, causing him to flake and itch constantly. By the light of the fire, he read books, scribbled shapes on the wall and watched the stars, meditating on their beauty.

His stomach growled, but he didn't move. He knew the pantry was completely empty. He could see inside it from his seat on the floor. He had torn off the door, using it and the shelves to feed his fire. Nothing remained in any of his open-faced cabinets.

His belly roared again and the room spun. He walked through the now door-less doorway to his backyard. A light covering of frost twinkled in the moonlight.

"Beautiful," he said aloud. His stomached growled and he asked it, "You agree?"

It growled again.

"Well, I'm sorry, buddy, but it's like this. I can't take anything new. It causes trouble, see? The stories I could tell you."

As if it didn't hear, his stomach bellowed again.

"What's that?" Joe hunched down. A scratching noise was coming from the pantry. He sat perfectly still. He shushed his belly as it gurgled again. Something was moving along the baseboards. Joe watched and waited, brushing his greasy hair from his eyes.

A tiny rat was sniffing its way around the walls, occasionally turning back, moving with the nervous twitching of a rodent exploring new territory.

Joe leaned forward, not making a sound. He crouched in the darkness. The rat stepped out of the pantry area and into the moonlight. Joe pounced on him.

The rat squealed and squiggled in Joe's hands. He almost lost him but caught him again.

"You have to understand," he told the rat, as the creature twitched and squirmed. "I can't buy food, so I have to get my own. It's so I never have to ask, 'Where did this come from?'"

Joe found a piece of wood with a sharp end from the chair he had destroyed. He pinned the rat on the floor with one hand, raising his makeshift dagger with the other. The rat squeaked. Joe's eyes flared.

"I promise I'll make it quick," he said.

4

Teri pushed herself up on one elbow, squinting in the light. Billy was standing in her bedroom doorway, leaning against the doorframe. He was a black figure, the light in the hall behind him casting his shadow forward. His bedroom wastebasket dangled from his hand.

"Billy? Why aren't you in bed, honey?"

"I can't sleep."

"Can't or don't want to?" She flicked on her bedside light.

"I'll sleep when I'm dead. Which will be soon enough."

Teri leapt from the bed and slapped him.

"Don't talk like that!"

The white afterimage of her fingers took their time refilling with the natural tone of his skin. He bowed his head.

"I'm sorry, honey," she said.

"It's all right," he sighed heavily. "I know this is harder on you than it is on me."

"What are you doing with your trash can?"

"I've been sick to my stomach," he held out the plastic bag-lined wastebasket. "See? I've been puking."

As he moved the can into the light, she could see the clumps of food were moist and black red. He was coughing up blood.

She gasped reflexively, her hand rising to her mouth. "Get your clothes on. Now. We're going to the clinic."

5

The Palaguan mine architect stared out the window across Palagua City. The sun was high in the sky, pounding heat down on the endless horizon of buildings. He patted the air conditioner window unit that roared next to his desk, thankful for the priceless appliance. This was the first summer in his life that his clothes didn't stick to his skin. Having grown up in Palagua, he never knew a summer could be so comfortable. He leaned back in his office chair, letting the cool breeze blow over his face.

He recalled the grueling days when he was a young man, struggling to earn his degree, working ten hours loading fruit onto trucks and attending Palagua University classes for another four hours, then collapsing onto the folded cardboard that passed for his bed. This air conditioner, one of probably only a thousand in all of Palagua City, made that effort worthwhile.

He was snapped out of his thoughts by his cell phone. The chirping device was another perk, but not nearly as wonderful as the air conditioner. The tiny screen indicated a message was waiting for him. He listened to the message. He played it again. Then again.

He dialed a number.

"Is this correct?"

"Is what correct?"

"The most recent... ah... work order. It says, 'Start plans for mining on the south side of the mountain.' But we're already mining on the north and east. The west side borders the river. The Huapi live on the south side."

His boss cleared his throat. "The Huapi are not your concern."

"I thought the guard had been sufficiently avenged."

"Security issues are not your job."

The mine architect held his cell phone away from him and rubbed his eyes.

"What's this all about?"

"What do you think?" came the angry reply. "It's about meeting increasing demand. Your job, as it always has been, is to plan the operation, draw up charts and maps. Concentrate on the fact that they want to mine the south side as well."

He crossed himself to boost his courage. "But sir, and of course I mean no disrespect, but to devise a plan like that would require that the Huapi no longer be there."

"That's the scenario we want you to work with," the tinny voice snapped. "They want more. We'll give them more."

"But sir, of course I am thankful for my job. Of course I am thankful for this, but this... Sir, they are innocents."

The line had gone dead. He was talking to himself. He turned the air conditioner off. A chill slithered over his skin.

6

Nina woke up, her entire body sore. She had been sleeping directly on the soft dirt and still had not become used to it. Ndiko lay snoring beside her. She stepped over him gingerly and sat on a log, staring towards the stench and clang of the mine.

The slaughter was several days past now, the last body long cremated and given up to the river. She sat among the demolished huts, looking around at the scattered remaining Huapi. They numbered less than twenty, most of them elderly.

They went about their routines in a pitiful attempt at defiance, trying to appear as if all was normal while the mechanical thunder of a full-scale drilling operation split the air and shook the earth with its noise.

Food gathering now involved collecting fruit from the jungle floor, where it had been jostled free by the constant vibration. Hunting required traveling far from the village to get meat, which the remaining men did only just before sunset. There were no fish in the river, the run-off from the mine had choked them all to death.

Nina had never felt so tired. "What am I doing here?" she asked herself.

Another truck bounced down the road, shaking the earth beneath her. She coughed as she yawned in a mouthful of fumes.

Ndiko stirred from his sleep, choking. He spat and sat down next to her. They rested their heads against each other.

"I wake up each day and you are here," he said. "Why do you stay?"

She took a long time to answer. "I'm not sure. Partly because I'm hiding from the police. I tried to damage one of the mining vehicles, and I injured some miners."

Ndiko raised his eyebrows and looked at her. "You never told me that before."

"We've been busy with," she paused, "with the burials."

"Yes." He hung his head. "You could leave," he said. "Leave and never come back. They are surely going to finish us off soon. We are doomed."

"I could leave," she said.

"If you don't, you will probably die."

Nina shrugged. The thought of death terrified her, but she didn't want him to know that. She was too tired to care about anything right now.

He coughed. "I am going to command those of us who are left to go join Lord Lardesus. I hope you will leave as well."

"What about you?"

"I have to stay. Someone must."

"In some way, I understand. I guess that's why I'm still here."

The clacking sound of a jackhammer striking stone cut off their conversation.

Nina closed her eyes.

The jackhammer stopped for a moment.

Ndiko held his head. "Soon I'll be dead and I won't have to breathe the smoke or hear the noise. I'll be part of the jungle, until they take that too."

7

Teri pulled her car onto Joe's two-lanes-wide driveway. She drove slowly up the curve leading to his enormous, unused front porch. His car door was open slightly, keys still in the ignition. No interior lights were on, the battery long dead. She took his keys and gently closed the door.

She approached the expansive entrance, stunned again by its size. She and Billy had only been here once. That was just after he became a millionaire, she thought, when he was still the Joe we knew and loved, when he was still human.

The home was a huge building, far more than any one person could use. The nearest houses were barely visible in the distance, dotting the rolling hills. It was evening, but none of the lights inside Joe's place were on. The front yard's open gate swung in the breeze, combing over a light covering of frost. The sloppy exterior was an offensive contrast to the manicured divinity of the neighbors' yards. A dim light flickered inside and a giant shadow walked along the wall, pacing.

She pushed open the unlocked front door. Her footsteps echoed in the vast, dark entry chamber. Something was burning. A faint, obsessive mumbling came from the nearby living room. The once pristine white walls were covered with writings in charcoal.

"No more!" was scribbled on the walls. "It's not my fault!" was written a hundred times, each entry numbered, like a child punished at school. The sequence jumped from ninety-nine to one million. Arching over the entire display was an angrily scribbled, "What can one person do? Jack Squat Nothing!"

Teri quietly closed the door behind her, using her feet to kick away the debris covering the floor. The mumbling from the other room stopped for a second, then picked up again.

"Joe?" she called.

There was a scuffling, a scrambling, a crash. Joe's voice boomed, "Who is it? I don't want to talk to the media!"

"Joe, it's me."

"I've got a gun!"

"Joe! It's Teri! Remember?"

"Teri? Teri. Teri," he mumbled, and began shuffling again. "Do I know a Teri? I don't even know myself. Who knew I would be a destroyer? It's not my fault! Who am I anyway? I don't know. Who is Teri? Does she know?"

She peeked around the corner, horrified by the sight. The ashes of his furniture were piled in the center of the room. Skeletal remnants of chairs and couches poked up from a pepper-colored pile. Everything that had once been in the room had been sucked into the center, consumed by fire and turned to ash. The walls were written on to the point they seemed carelessly stroked with a thick black paint.

"Joe?" she whispered.

A naked primate, hunched over, whirled around, frightened eyes glistening in a face full of hair. As he spun, he sprayed off a cloud of dust. Insanity twinkled ominously in his eyes. She was sure they were Joe's eyes, but the man, the creature, behind them was a stranger.

"Oh, my God. Joe, it's me. Teri."

"Teri?" his rancid breath reached across the room, forcing her to step back. He tilted his head, curious. She smiled at him, pitifully.

"I don't really have a gun," he said, chuckling. "That would require buying something."

"Joe. Billy wants to see you. He's... He's running out of time."

Joe began pacing again. "Billy? I remember a Billy. I think. Good kid. Good kid. I think. Unlike me." He scratched his hair violently, raising a cloud of dandruff. "I'm bad. Bad! Bad!" He smacked himself on the head in time with his words.

"Joe?"

"It's not my fault!" he turned and screamed at her. "I didn't kill anyone! I didn't want it to happen!"

She yelled at him. "Joe! Stop it!"

He ignored her and began mumbling and pacing again.

Teri sighed. "Where is the bathroom? Because if I have an accident on your floor, it is definitely going to be your fault. Not that it really matters."

"It's back there," he pointed. "I haven't flushed, though. That wastes water. Or you can use the pit near the back porch."

"I'll try the bathroom." She headed in the direction he pointed. Each step felt like she was walking uphill, pushing through solid stench.

"You might think it smells," Joe called.

"Oh..." she choked back vomit burning her throat. "I'll go around back. You got any toilet paper?"

"No," he said, scrabbling through a pile of garbage, digging with his hands like a crazed rodent. "No need to buy anything. Paper kills trees. No need to kill trees. I use paperbacks. Trees already dead. Books already read. No more trees killed. Here."

Teri took the soiled, coverless paperback and examined it.

"The Collected Works of Ernest Hemingway," she said. "Hm. Close enough."

* * *

When she returned from relieving herself, Teri spoke sternly. "Joe, what is all this? What are you doing? What do you want to achieve?"

"No more consumption!" He grinned. "No more taking. I have everything I need and I know where it comes from. We're rich. We're all rich. This country has everything it needs. We all do. No need to take any more. I won't do it." He traced his fingers through the black sand at his feet.

"Joe, you're a skeleton. You need to eat."

"I'm fine! I've been eating grass and bugs and the occasional rat. I'm still alive. Collecting rainwater. Melting snow. Delicious. Natural. No need for a plastic bottle. Rain. Water. Drink. It's good. Natural. No plastic. Plastic supports oil supports war. It's all connected. Crystal Clay supports toys supports violence and death and cruelty and I didn't do it and I'm not going to be a part of it and I know I can't stop it but I won't do it anymore. All the same. It's all the same!"

He scratched his head furiously, loosening his hair, creating a faint pink friction-burn on his scalp.

Teri inhaled deeply. "Okay. Joe, if you're listening, if you're still in there, Billy wants to see you again. He's..." she cleared her throat, "not doing well."

"Billy." Teri noticed her son's name was the only thing that seemed to pause Joe's manic behavior.

"He misses you."

"I miss him. I miss you. I miss lots of things but I don't need them. Nope. There's a difference between need and want. Whatever I need, I take and no more. But I don't really need anything now. I'm rich. I want things but I don't take them. Of course I want the things I need, so maybe I should stop. Maybe I should stop drinking and eating then I'll stop shitting and I'll die and I won't need anything ever."

"I miss you, too, Joe. I need you. Things are rough."

He turned and yelled at her again. "It's not my fault!"

"No one says it is. You never intended for any of this to happen to those poor people in Palagua."

"No. I didn't. Palagua. Nice place. Nice people. I didn't do it. I didn't mean to. I just wanted to help."

Teri stormed across the room and grabbed his elbow, catching him mid-stride. "Joe! Don't flog yourself. This is ridiculous! Billy needs you."

"Needs me or wants me?" he snapped free of her grip and began his back and forth lumbering walk again.

"All right," she said, shouldering her purse, "Billy will probably have to go to the hospital to live soon. He misses you. You're the closest thing to a father he ever had. If you want to, come see him. Come see us." She handed him a slip of paper with Billy's room number and her phone numbers.

He stuffed it in his pocket without looking at it. "I'll keep it. It might make a good tissue. Amazing how many uses paper has. You can re-use it too. Did you know that?"

"It would be nice if I didn't have to go through this alone." She turned and left. Stopping at the door, she called back. "Joe, I could really use your help."

Joe grabbed a piece of charcoal and began scribbling on the wall, ignoring the sound of the door closing.

"Help. Help. That's all I wanted to do was help. But look now. Look what has happened. Help. Help. Help. Everybody wants help. Everybody needs help. If they need it, they want it. No need for want."

Later that night, Joe lay on his back on the hardwood floor, shivering but lacking a blanket. From the darkness he heard a tiny scratching, then silence. Another scratching noise, then silence. He lay still as he could, slowing his breathing. The scratching was next to his ear now. Suddenly, he felt a light weight on his chest as a squirrel leapt on him. He didn't move, letting the creature sniff, then scuttle across him, over his face, his stomach and down his leg. Joe didn't move at all, making no effort to catch and eat the animal. As quickly as he came, the squirrel leapt off Joe and skittered into the night.

"I don't need anything. See?" Joe said. His stomach growled. He punched it. "I said I don't need anything!"

8

"Scherr, we have to talk." The abrupt message sent a chill down Ethan's spine. He rubbed his sweaty palms on his tailored pants before he slowly walked to the MajorCo CEO's office door. "Sir, you wanted to see me?"

The CEO gestured. "Ethan! Come in, close the door. This is important."

Scherr's guard went up. His natural paranoia warned him that time alone with the boss usually meant a scolding. Or worse.

"Now, Ethan, I'm sure you feel you've done a good job."

"I think so. Sir," Scherr said, sitting up straight in his chair. Damn right, he thought, I've made this company.

"But I'm sure you understand that some decisions in business are extremely difficult."

"I do." This can't be happening, Scherr thought.

"And I'm sure you know that sometimes even top performers get the short end of the stick. Sometimes they have to be let go."

"I've heard." What the hell is going on here? Scherr wondered, as sweat formed in his armpits.

"Being a CEO means having to make decisions, sometimes even decisions I don't want to make, but that circumstance forces me into."

"Yes." He sounds like he's getting ready to fire me, Scherr thought. But he can't! His eye twitched. He ground his teeth.

"Well," the CEO shrugged and frowned. He tapped his fingertips together and looked down at his desk.

"Well," Scherr said.

Silence.

"Get to the point," Scherr growled.

The CEO looked up smiling. "You're good."

"Good?"

The smile grew wider. "Most people explode by now."

"What are you talking about?"

"It's a joke!" the CEO slapped his desktop. "I'm not going to fire you. Nothing bad is happening to you. In fact, I have very good news."

Scherr loosened his collar. "Remind me to never play you in poker. That was some act. So what's the news?"

The CEO reached into his desk drawer and removed a cigar case. He flipped it open, lit up and offered one. "These are worth more than most people make in a year. Only the best for a newly promoted member of our executive team."

"Excuse me?" Scherr asked, surprised, his eyes flying wide open.

The CEO smiled.

"No joke?"

"No joke."

"No kidding."

"No kidding. You've made the difference with this company, my friend. Now sit down and enjoy a smoke. Let's put work aside and just talk."

Scherr stood to look out over the city from the huge window.

The CEO rose from his chair and clapped him on the shoulder. "Welcome to the top, Ethan Scherr. I take it you like the view?"

"Very much, sir," Ethan smiled. "I like it very much."

Part 12

1

Teri bit the side of her tongue as she watched Billy struggle to open his present. He could barely sit up in the hospital bed he was so tethered down by the web of tubes connecting to him. His bone-thin arms shook as they moved.

"For God's sake," she thought. "Please."

The chubby baby boy she once ran with was now a working skeleton, struggling to tear apart wrapping paper.

"I'm so weak," Billy whined, collapsed back onto the bed, the paper still whole.

"Here, let me help," Teri said, pulling at the wrapping.

Beneath the paper was a box, covered with photos of his school class in different activities. Each student had signed the box and handwritten get-well-soon cards.

"That's nice," Teri said. "Look what they made for you."

"Yeah, it's okay."

"Are you going to open it?"

"I wish I could."

"Here, I'll do it."

Her son watched as she slowly folded back the four-panel lid of the package. Inside were more wrapped presents, all different shapes and sizes.

"More presents!" Teri exclaimed.

"Great. More things I can't open," he turned his head to the side and stared out the window at the city skyline. He coughed out a chuckle.

"Now, Billy."

"Mom, if I can't laugh now, when am I going to?"

"Here, I'll just take this first one."

"Better hurry, I don't have a lot of time."

"Stop it."

Teri opened the first present. It was a deck of cards.

"That's nice," she said. "We can play cards. You love games."

Billy said nothing.

Teri opened another present; it was a comic book. "Oh, look at this! Heroes of Mythology. Very nice."

"I've already read that one."

Teri slammed her hands down. "Billy, I'm trying. I need you to do the same."

Billy stretched out his slender hand and touched the cover of the comic book.

Teri reached into the care package and brought out another present. She opened it silently, and set it down without a word. It was a Crystal Clay toy. A rounded star-shaped crystal glowed, caged between a piece of cardboard and molded plastic.

"Wow, I can't wait to show Joe that one," Billy said. "That is, if he shows up before I'm worm-food."

Teri stared at him, too furious to speak. Her cheeks flushed and her eyes filled with tears.

"I wonder who gave me that," he said. "I bet it was Cory. If only I knew the Huapi word for moron."

Teri threw down the care package and looked away.

"Presents don't mean anything, Mom. I want to get up. But I can't do anything."

She stood and stormed out of his room, out of the hospital, shoving the door hard. Three young interns in their pale aqua scrubs were smoking under a tree. She borrowed a cigarette and sat on a bench, staring at the ground as she smoked, too tired to cry.

2

The remainder of the Huapi tribe gathered around a fire. Ten Huapi, including Ndiko, were left; with Nina they were eleven.

A pipe was lit and passed. Nina took a deep drag. The sounds of the mine drifted away, becoming less of a bother. They sounded like drunk animals, she thought, hilarious naked drunk animals having a party. She giggled and passed the pipe to Ndiko.

"Good stuff," she said in English, out of habit. She could feel the burning herb snaking through her veins, relaxing her.

Ndiko looked at her, confused. She translated.

"It's a saying from America. That's all."

Ndiko stared at the ground thoughtfully. "Tell us more about the tribe from America. I am unable to understand these people. The Palaguans take the gods' gift from us and sell it to these Americans. Why do they want it so badly? Why do they want so much of it? Did their gods not give them any gifts? Is America a land of cruel people?" The rest of the circle waited for her answer, listening intently.

Nina chose her words carefully. "Cruel? No. I wouldn't say that. The tribe is very large. When everyone in America wants something, that adds up to a lot. Individually, most of the people are not greedy, but as a whole they are."

"So each person thinks themselves innocent," Ndiko said. "Strange how so much innocence can add up to so much evil. It is like rain, a single drop makes no difference, but a large amount can move the world."

"Correct."

"So this America's desire is just like the forces of the jungle. Like rain, a river, a flood. I cannot stop it, I cannot fight it, I cannot change it. I simply must learn to deal with it."

"That's correct," Nina said, taking another drag. "So, what do you plan to do?"

"I plan to live as a Huapi until they come here and kill us all." He smirked at her, his eyes bloodshot. "I will let the river drown me. What else can I do?"

"I don't know. You could leave."

"No. I cannot. If a flood were to come or a fire to consume us, we would have no choice but to deal with it. The end would be here. All that is left is to reflect on my life."

Nina realized only her and Ndiko were talking, the rest of the tribe listening. She felt self-conscious for a moment, but the herb pushed the feeling down.

"So, Ndiko," she said, "As you reflect, do you have any regrets?"

"Sometimes I think I should have killed you and your friend when you were saving my father's life. Then I would have lost my father and I would have lost you, but I would have saved our whole tribe. When I'm dead, I'll no longer have to think about it."

"Well," Nina said, "I know I'm biased, but let me say I'm glad you didn't kill me."

"I am, too. Looking back it seems I couldn't have it both ways. I wanted to save everyone, but each path had a price."

"America has a saying for that: 'Damned if you do, damned if you don't.'"

"What does this mean?"

"It means no matter what you do, or even if you do nothing, you are made to suffer. You are sent to sent to a place called hell, a place of infinite sorrow and suffering. We call it damned."

"It sounds like here and now. Are we, as you say, damned?"

They both burst out laughing. "Being damned can occur anywhere I guess."

"You know a lot of sayings," Ndiko said. "The only one I know is the Huapi phrase, 'Where did this come from?'"

"It's a good saying," Nina said. "Very thoughtful."

"Thoughtful, but not very useful. I think 'damned' explains the world better."

3

"Show us what you have so far," the boss commanded.

The Palaguan architect's hands shook. He had been stalling. He had claimed he was sick, claimed the job was too difficult, claimed his daughter was sick, then his wife. He held out as long as he dared, delaying the inevitable, because he simply could not afford to lose his job. He tried to convince himself it was not his fault, that he was just doing as instructed, but he still felt guilty.

Now his boss and several other suits had all shown up without warning at his office. One was the American Ambassador, another the Palaguan National Exports Minister.

"God forgive me," the architect mumbled to himself as he laid out the plans. He stretched a large map over the table and brushed it down, breathing deeply before he continued. "The mine can move here, but we would need to level all of this forest. From that angle, rather than transport down the road, it would be more beneficial to deliver supplies from and receive harvests at the river, but that would require eliminating this part of the jungle as well."

The Ambassador and the Exports Minister reviewed the concept and nodded their approval. "Looks great. Good job," the American said, slapping him on his back.

"There is the small problem of the Huapi village," the architect whimpered. "I recommend relocation."

"But they live in the jungle," the American stated.

"Yes."

"So if we plow over where they're living now, they'll just move to another part of the jungle, right? I mean, we're not killing the rainforest, we're just using part of it."

The architect ignored the glares from his fellow Palaguans. "This area is their land, it is bordered by the city and the river. Once we level this area, there will be nowhere for them to go."

"That's not true, is it?" the American said, looking around the room. "They're people, they're not stupid. They'll find somewhere to live, right?"

"Of course, my friend," the Exports Minister said. "They have already left the area. There is no one there. We have already taken care of it."

"Oh good," the Ambassador said, leaning over the plans again, "because that was all news to me."

The architect said nothing more about the Huapi until his bedtime prayers, where he begged their souls for forgiveness.

* * *

"Sir, it's a call from Palagua."

Ethan Scherr nodded to his assistant and picked up the phone. He listened very carefully.

"The whole area," the caller said. "This will mean, um, that, um, no one will be able to live there, and any creature living there will have to be chased out or..." the voice trailed off.

Scherr held his breath, before speaking. "We have to meet demand. Do it."

"Understood, sir. We will, immediately."

"Hang on a second." Scherr rose from his desk and paced, rubbing his head. "At least give them a warning."

"That can be arranged."

The call ended.

Scherr stared out at the city skyline.

"Well, Vera," he sighed, "I guess you had a point all along."

4

Teri knew everything immediately, without a word being spoken. She knew immediately when the doctor came in the room, accompanied by a woman in a flower-print dress and sweater. She wore a small badge on her shirt that simply read, "Social Worker."

"I'm sorry," the doctor began, and Teri guessed correctly everything he was going to say after that. She caught only the key words. She had gone through it all before with her father, the script concerning terminal cancer patients was a memorable one.

"Spreading... Inoperable... Quality of life... What's best for him..."

The social worker pushed a booklet across the table to her. "Learning to Let Go," the cover read. The border was in lavender, framing a photo of flowers in a meadow, the sun setting in the background.

"Is Billy's father around?" the social worker asked. She smiled gently. It was a question Teri hadn't anticipated.

"His father and I haven't spoken in years," she said. "I have no idea where he is."

"Billy has mentioned a Joe before. A family friend?"

"Yes."

"It might be nice for Billy if Joe were to visit."

"I'll see what I can do. We haven't seen him in a while, either."

The doctor reached out to her and firmly grasped her hand. "I understand this is a tough time. I can't imagine what you're going through. Let me know if you think there's anything we can get for you."

"Thanks," she said, impressed with how well she was taking it. The lack of surprise made all the difference.

Joe woke up on the floor of his mansion and looked around, grunting as he pushed himself up to a sitting position.

He slowly panned his gaze left and right across his destroyed home. Black-grey skeletons of rats and squirrels were stacked in the corner under a cloud of flies. Several buckets were set out on his porch to collect rain. He could see them through the doorway where he had removed the door and demolished it for firewood. In the room's center was a pile of ash. Nearly everything he owned had been burned to provide energy, for cooking and staying warm.

He looked down at his chest. His ribs pushed through his greenish flesh. His pants were sliding down his waist, exposing his hip bones. He no longer seemed to have skin on his hands. They were skeletal claws, covered with mud, dried blood and cinder.

The sun tracked across the room slowly, marking time. After hours of silent observation of himself and his environment, he finally drew his conclusion.

"This is ridiculous," he said aloud.

He stood up, his muscles shaking from the effort. "What the hell am I doing?"

He waited there a long time, standing, swaying with weakness, watching the sun continue to move across his soot-covered floor. He ran his fingers over his chest, strumming on his ribs. "How did I get here?"

He looked around his place, "Where did this all come from?"

As he recalled the Huapi phrase, he remembered. He replayed the entire saga in his head, curled up in the fetal position in his burned out mansion, and bawled for hours, wailing and shivering.

As the sun dipped to the edge of the frost-covered horizon, the crunching sound of a car rolled up his driveway. He roughly wiped away his tears as someone entered the front door. Footsteps approached. He didn't move or call out. Teri rounded the corner and without a word, she tossed him a greasy bag of fast food. It smelled rich, like a super-food, so full of fat and protein he felt he could live off it for a month. This was what he used to eat for just for one meal?

His hands grabbed at the food and he bit into it, taking a piece out of the thin wrapper as well. He devoured the burger like the starving man he was, nearly biting off his own fingers as he chewed.

"This is the last time I'm visiting," she said. "If Joe is still in there, behind that beard, under the dirt, I hope he hears me. Billy is running out of time. He's done with treatment. We give up. I give up."

Joe looked up, confused, a hunk of bun hanging from his mouth.

"He's going to die," Teri said, anger holding back her tears. "Soon. He always asks about you. I tell him you're away on business and he knows I'm lying. Maybe if you can grow up, you could find some time to stop by. But if you can't get yourself together, don't bother. He's already had one bum for a father figure. He doesn't need another."

She turned, kicking aside debris.

"Wait," Joe called out.

"Make it quick," she said, turning back.

"Don't you understand why I did this?"

"I think so, Joe. The question is, do I care? Does Billy care? Did you prove a point? Are you proud? Could you show yourself to Billy as you are and feel like you made the world a better place?"

Joe said nothing, he just kept chewing. The first burger was gone. He attacked the second.

Teri continued, "I get your point here, Joe. We consume too much. We live too extravagant in this country. The Huapi and who knows who else suffer because of it. I got it. And you're right. Fine. Definitely we need a diet, but what you've done here, this is something else. More like anorexia."

Joe kept chewing. The burger was the best thing he had ever eaten in his life. He didn't care where it came from, or how it was obtained. He wanted it, needed it. Food meant everything.

"I don't have the answers," Teri said. "But did this help? Did your Huapi friends get their land? Did they come back to life? I don't know how to fix it, Joe. You can't unless you could somehow get everyone uninterested at the same time, and that's impossible. I just came by to ask you, beg you, for Billy's sake. One more visit. Before..."

She paused, gathering her strength. She sighed as she said it.

"Before he dies."

"I'm trying-" Joe said, talking with his mouth full.

"You're trying to do the impossible. While you're making your point, life goes on. I don't want to talk anymore, Joe. Time's up. Goodbye."

"Teri, please."

She left.

6

The television:

Three men in suits sat around a table. The speaker on the right was set against a red background, under the word "Right." The speaker on the left sat in front of a blue background, under the word "Left." Thick, squat letters spelling "Perspectives" ran down the middle of the set, a border into which the host's seat was very carefully placed.

Left pushed his glasses up his nose. "The Huapi people are losing their-"

Right interrupted. "I'm sick of this politically correct bull. So the kids like the Crystal Clay. If those Hoopees just realized how much their natural resource is under demand, they could be living in mansions instead of grass huts. No one wants to destroy their land or hurt them. The smiles on our children's faces were worth it."

"All I'm saying is that we need to acknowledge that people suffer to bring us-"

"Now, wait a minute," the host said. "Wait your turn."

"Sure," Right said, "Acknowledged. Now who cares? Stop trying to be such a stick in the mud. For God's sake, if it were up to you, no one would ever have any fun. That's what I despise about the leftist perspective. Sure some people suffered."

"Some people died. I'd like to-" Left said.

Right talked over him. "What about all the parents who suffered to bring home the money to buy those toys? They don't want to hurt anybody, they just want one. Those are the letters I get. 'I don't want a lot, just my share.' Just to make their children happy. Is that so wrong?"

Left turned his head to the side.

The host spoke up. "Left? Do you want to say something? I'm giving you the floor."

Left did not respond.

"Hello?"

"This show is crap," Left said. "I can't get a word in." He unclipped his collar microphone and spiked it. He stormed off the set.

The host and Right shrugged. "Well, I guess the show is all yours."

"I guess so. As I was saying, everyone wants to talk about rights. What about our rights as consumers?"

7

Night in the jungle usually struck Nina as a time of beauty and peace. Living in the Huapi village, night was now awful.

She yanked down her pants, leaned against a tree, and stuck her rear behind her as far as she could. Pain seized her belly as diarrhea erupted loudly into a pit she had dug. The sensation felt like her stomach leaking out. Acid burned her insides as she wiped herself with the leaves Ndiko had told her to use.

When it was over, she covered the pit while trucks rumbled nearby. As a sort of statement, the Huapi had shifted their latrine-area dangerously close to the mining road.

She made her way back to the ruined village, holding her stomach.

"You're not kidding," she said to Ndiko. "Even with the purification pills, that water is poison."

The Huapi gathered around the fire laughed at her.

"Now you're a true Huapi," Ndiko said. "Welcome to the tribe."

The Huapi chuckled half-heartedly.

Floodlights illuminating the mine filled the night sky with a haze that obscured most of the stars. The hiss and clang of machines and the shouting of men working nearly clashed with their fireside talk.

Still, the Huapi tradition lived on, gathering around the nightly fire, passing the pipe, blowing away the day's worries in a smoky stupor.

"We are the last of the Huapi," one of the older survivors said before he took a puff.

"It's an honor to be among you," Nina said.

"Why not make her one of us?" someone asked.

The others chimed in. "Great idea. We need to replace everyone who has left. She's had the runs, she's one of us. We don't do much else anymore."

They all laughed hysterically as the herb they were smoking tickled their brains.

"We need as many as we can get," Ndiko agreed.

Nina blushed. "Can you make me a Huapi?"

"I can do anything. I'm chief!"

"How do you do it? What do I have to do?"

"First, you have to understand that Huapi men are especially needy in the morning," one of the women said. The ladies laughed, the men frowned good-naturedly.

A truck's air-horn blared, stopping all conversation for a moment.

"If you're going to be a Huapi woman, you'll have to learn to cry until you get your way," one of the men said. It was their turn to laugh.

"So, what do I have to do?" she asked Ndiko.

His eyes narrowed mischievously. "You must look at me."

She did. He placed his hand in front of her face and gently tapped her on the forehead. "There, now you're a Huapi."

"It's a pleasure!" she said. The pipe was handed across the circle to her and she took a deep drag.

"Thank you. It's an honor."

A truck rumbled by, spewing exhaust. The whole village was absorbed into the dark cloud. They all fell over with delirious, hopeless laughter, coughing, tears running down their faces.

Part 13

1

"I'm here to see a William Young. He's checked in for pediatric cancer."

Joe squinted at the clinic's harsh fluorescent lights, but still couldn't get used to them. He couldn't get used to anything. The drive to the hospital had been a thrill ride, all speed and thunder. Computer screens were like fluid paper. After his time living as a primitive man, nothing about high-tech modern life seemed normal.

"Mister Vera, this way, please."

He rubbed his newly-shaved chin as he followed the nurse down a corridor past brightly-colored rooms. Children were playing with toys, watching television, attended to by lively nurses. It could have been any daycare center in the world, with one difference: these children were sprouting a multitude of mechanical and chemical attachments. Almost all of them were bald.

The worst part of it was the lack of speed and sound. Being around children was always a fast-moving activity, as the urge to play overtook them. Not here. These children lived in ravaged bodies, eroded by disease and medicine warring inside them. They were subdued, stoned on meds, barely able to walk. A crying woman stroked a child's arm as the pre-schooler dozed on a couch.

Joe looked away and kept walking.

"Right here," the nurse said, indicating an open door.

Joe felt as though he were moving in slow motion.

First he saw the bland wall. Then the television. Then the end of the bed, a lump where two small feet hid under the covers.

He heard Teri and Billy talking. He took a deep breath and rounded the corner.

Even moving slowly, he was unprepared. He let out an involuntary gasp.

Billy looked more like a machine than a boy. Wires crawled around his bald head, stuck there by white adhesive circles. An IV-stand rose near his arm, and several beeping and chirping machines sat on a shelf.

"Joe!" the boy-machine croaked, smiling crookedly. He sounded drunk on painkillers, his eyes focusing poorly as he attempted to rise.

A part of Joe died then. Somewhere inside him, he felt a piece of his soul break off and fall away. The effort Billy gave to his smile was so valiant, so hopeless. Joe imagined his own smile must look the same.

* * *

They talked about ancient Greek and Roman mythology.

Billy pointed, a needle in his arm, to his large colorful graphic novel about Hercules, narrating each scene. He treated Joe as if he had never left.

Finally the boy leaned back, exhausted, and closed his eyes. Without a sound, he fell asleep.

Teri and Joe left the room. The sun was still high in the sky.

"How long was that?" Joe asked. "It seemed like all day, but it's still light out."

"It was only a couple hours."

"Really? Time seemed..."

"Slow. I know. And when it's over, it will seem so fast."

"Teri. Don't talk like that."

She fished in her pocket for a pack of cigarettes. "Give me this, Joe. Just the truth. I'm facing so much now, and losing so much, let me at least have the truth. I don't have time for anything less."

He said nothing more as they exited the hospital and took their seats on a bench.

Teri smoked in long desperate drags.

"I'm glad you came," she said as she exhaled.

"I should have been here sooner."

"You should have."

They sat in silence.

"Anything we can do for him?" Joe said. "Anything special? I'd spend every last penny I have."

"I can't think of anything right now, let alone be creative." She took another enormous drag and held it a long time before exhaling.

2

"Man of the Year!" the cover of the business magazine screamed in bold, extruded, superhero letters. Ethan Scherr stood legs apart, hands on hips, his hair and suit rippling under the pressure of a strong wind.

Subheadings listed Ethan's accomplishments: "From obscure to top shelf!" "The Overnight Executive" and "Ethan Scherr puts the Major in MajorCo Toys!"

Scherr leaned back in his chair and stared at the wall with the framed poster-sized blow up of the cover. He smiled.

He admired the view of the city beneath him.

"You did it, Ethan. You did it," he said to himself.

3

"I'm going to leave tonight," Nina said to Ndiko, as the nightly smoking session around the fire began.

"Just for tonight?" he asked. "You're going to come back?"

"I want to get something from my old home."

"I'm sorry our village has become so repulsive."

"It's- Trust me, I'll return."

The Huapi exchanged looks, skeptical. "You're not coming back," one of the elders snorted. Ndiko turned and walked away.

"I'll be back," she said. "I promise."

No one acknowledged her.

* * *

The hike was much smoother than she expected. Living with the Huapi the past few weeks had paid off in lost pounds. The moon was high when she reached her apartment. A sign was posted on the door that it was sealed by order of the revolutionary government.

She scanned the area, listening. There were no suspicious sounds, only the usual rustling of the night wind in the trees. The night was late enough for her neighbors to still be out dancing or listening to music, but not so late that people were staggering home drunk, singing and yelling. The alley that led to her home was empty.

She touched her front door and was not surprised to find the lock had been pried loose.

As she expected, the place had been ransacked, probably by the police and later by their friends. That much she expected. What surprised her was the fact that she wasn't that upset about it. She knocked on the floor around the area where her bed had been (it had been tilted over, its ancient mattress stolen.) She pushed one of the floorboards up and pulled out her tiny strong box with the combination lock.

She opened it and found her valuables: her passport, some Palaguan cash, her mother's wedding ring, and her digital camera. She pocketed the items and left her old home, taking one last look. She left the door open, blowing in the breeze.

* * *

The sun was rising when she neared the Huapi village.

She approached quietly.

Ndiko was pacing.

She watched from a distance. He still hadn't seen her.

His brow was tense, staring intently at the ground before him. He clenched and released his spear, clearly worried. About her?

"Ndiko," she called as she neared him.

"Nina!" He turned quickly, sprinting toward her. He slowed and composed himself. "Are you okay?" he asked.

"Yes. I'm fine. You?"

"The same."

"Did you miss me?" she asked playfully.

He squinted at her, confused. "I did. You are all I have left now."

She smiled. "You are all I have, too."

"That's not true," he said. "You still have a world you could return to if you wanted."

"I've left it."

They stared at each other, neither one budging.

"What did you leave for?" he asked.

She smiled and shrugged, but didn't answer.

4

Joe and Teri were crowded around Billy's bed, all three of them watching the TV news. The reports were the same they were everywhere, as they had always been. Somewhere some people killed some other people. Somewhere a car accident killed people. Somewhere a plane crashed and killed people. Somewhere a bomb went off and killed people.

"Why so much death? So much violence?" Billy asked, his voice woozy.

Teri and Joe looked at each other, silently willing the other to field the question. Joe took it.

"I don't know, Ace," he said. "Some people are cruel, some are angry, some are oppressed. Lots of reasons. None of them all that great."

"I'd like to tell them all that it's silly."

"You would?" Teri asked.

"Yes. I'd like to get on the television and ask everyone to be kind to each other. To just stop killing each other. For just one day."

Teri looked to Joe and he looked back to her.

"Well, why don't you?" Joe said.

Billy understood quickly. "Would you? Could you? Can you pay for it?"

"We can look into it," Teri said, patting his knee.

"Thanks," Billy said. He leaned back and fell asleep, a weak smile on his face.

"You were going to show me something," Ndiko said.

"Tonight. Around the fire," Nina replied.

"But I'm the chief. And you are Huapi now, you must do what I say," he said, smirking.

"Things have changed."

Ndiko frowned. "Nothing is as it was."

That night, he turned to her as soon as the pipe was lit.

"So, when I am dead, will you tell your fellow pales what they have done to my people?"

"We've been trying to tell them. Some listen, most don't. We tried. Joe and I tried."

"Joe did?"

"Yes. He felt terrible and he has tried to stop our people from ruining your land."

Ndiko thought about this. "Perhaps I was too hard on him."

"Perhaps we both were."

They were silent for a long time.

Nina summoned her courage and pulled her digital camera from her pocket. "This is what I wanted to show you. This is how I will help Joe tell them."

"By showing them a silver box?"

"It's more than that. Smile."

"What for?"

"Smile."

He forced a smile. She raised the camera to her eye.

"What are you doing?"

The flash made him leap in the air. He landed, spear in his hands, crouched in a defensive position. The other Huapi scurried away from the fire.

"The people on the boat had that!" Ndiko screamed. "The box that flashes! What did you do to me? What have you done?"

"Nothing. Calm down. You're fine. Look." She set her camera on preview. Ndiko took a horrible picture, his smile stiff and uncertain, his eyes closed.

"Look," she said, turning the camera in her hand so he could see the screen. She turned it toward the others. They squinted at it, amazed and frightened.

Ndiko cautiously approached the camera, spear between him and it. He tilted his head back and forth.

"It's me," he reached out to touch it. "There's my spear!"

"That's right," she said. "And I can-"

"No, wait, let me try again!" he struck an angry pose, bared his teeth and raised his spear.

She snapped a picture and showed him the screen.

"Look at me!" he laughed. "I'm ferocious!"

"It's about time," one of the elders joked.

Ndiko ignored the barb. "It's so... so... there are no Huapi words to say it! It's beautiful!"

"Cool." Nina said, in English. "Cool."

"Cool," Ndiko said, pronouncing his first English word. "Cool. Cool."

He switched back to Huapi and reached for the camera. "Let me see my fierce picture again."

She laughed and showed him. "And look, I can show you other pictures."

She hit a button on the camera and cycled through the pictures on the camera's memory. His mouth hung open with wonder as she showed him her photography collection. Flowers here, scenes from the market, caimans in shallow water.

Ndiko touched the camera reverently, whispering, "It's a whole world in there."

She continued cycling, finally coming to the only picture she had taken the fateful day on the tour boat, when Joe had saved Chief Maubombo's life and the end of the Huapi began.

"Stop!" Ndiko yelled. "Father!"

He grabbed the camera from her and touched the tiny screen. It showed his father, Chief Maubombo, his fist in the air on the beach, cursing the tour boat that disturbed the peace of his land.

"It's my father!" he cried to Nina. "Can this magic box get him out? Father!" He yelled at the camera as if yelling to someone in the distance.

"Ndiko," she said. "It's not him. It's just a picture of him."

Ndiko cradled the camera delicately in his hands. "It's like my father lives, in here. Not really lives, but lives in the way memories live."

"Exactly."

"It's like he's not dead. Like he's immortal! Look, everyone!"

Nina began to realize how much she'd always taken photos for granted.

The Huapi passed the camera from person to person. "Maubombo," they whispered.

"Look at him!" Ndiko held the camera high above his head, then looked at it so closely his nose was touching the screen, then he extended his arm and squinted at the picture, then brought it close again. Nina watched him with the same fascination he watched the camera.

"Father," he whispered. He smiled sadly and continued to stare. Hours passed as they smoked. Ndiko fell asleep with the camera still in his hands.

6

Joe shook his head. Being rich was like being in another world. Before he had his money, if he had called a television station and said, "I know a young boy who is dying. His last wish is to go on television and beg for world peace. I'm willing to pay," they would have laughed at him.

Instead, when he mentioned his name and how his money came to him, they were suspicious, but there was a definite respect in their tone. Now, Joe realized, it was actually going to happen. Billy was going to film a television spot and speak about world peace. The days since the idea had started had flown by. He and Teri leapt into the project, finally having something to do other than watch her boy die.

A charity that helped terminally-ill children fulfill their final wishes had been contacted by the television station's production team as potential co-sponsors. Joe refused the offer but did provide the group with an advertising spot after Billy's speech. He gave them a healthy donation to use in Billy's name.

The cancer was obviously taking Billy now. Joe and Teri had finally caught up to Billy in their acceptance. They no longer dwelled on it, but they all knew he was winding down.

Billy used every moment he was awake and lucid to compose his speech. He even seemed to revive against the illness, but they kept a check on their hopes.

Acceptance had been so hard to come by, they were careful not to destroy it with hope.

Joe rested his hand protectively on the boy's shoulder as the camera crews set up at the foot of the bed.

A woman ("Call me Miss Janey") from the TV station's public relations department fluttered around the room, tending to everyone, a hummingbird with a clipboard.

Joe frowned at the cameras and sound equipment. There was already enough machinery around Billy. The set up was just adding to it.

"Joe," Billy said.

"What's up, Ace?"

"I'm a little nervous."

Joe and Teri laughed.

"Just be yourself, kid. Everyone likes you."

Billy nodded.

"You'll do fine," Teri added.

"You ready for your make-up?" Miss Janey asked.

"Bring it on," Billy smiled.

* * *

After Billy's make-up was applied, Joe asked everyone except Teri to leave the room. The crew shrugged and agreed.

"Time is important," Miss Janey reminded them on her way out.

"What's going on?" Billy asked as Teri gently closed the door.

"I have something to give you," Joe said.

He reached deep into his pocket and removed a piece of Crystal Clay. Unshaped by MajorCo Toys' manufacturing division, the stone cast wild rainbows about the room. "For good luck."

"But I don't want any Crystal Clay," Billy said. Teri frowned, worried.

"Billy. I promised," Joe said, "And it took me some doing, and the hiring of some very mean lawyers in secret. Even though it wasn't in our original agreement, I got this back from MajorCo Toys. This is the only piece of Crystal Clay that was freely given out by the Huapi people. I promised you I would get it back and I did. I wanted to surprise you."

Billy hesitated before taking it. "You sure it's the original?"

"See for yourself."

Billy took it and turned it in his hands, feeling every edge of the rock. He closed his eyes and felt it again while explaining, "I used to hold it while I was in bed, in the dark."

As gaunt as he was, his smile was robust as the crystal passed its ultimate test. "There was a dent right here and further up, a sharp edge – here!" Billy's voice was racing. "And here there's two nicks. Joe!" He yelled, as much as he could, his eyes flying wide open. "Thank you!"

Joe leaned over and gave him a hug, trying to ignore the fact that he could feel the little boy's bones.

* * *

Teri opened the door and allowed the herd of TV people back in. Miss Janey smiled at Joe and Teri, and seeing their moist eyes, offered a tissue to both. As the cameras were given a final check, Joe placed the Crystal Clay near Billy's head on the pillow and nodded to the cameraman.

Billy read from the cards weakly, softly. The director praised him and gave advice: "Don't slur your words. Try to say every one distinct and separate."

Billy performed four takes before he collapsed on the pillow. The director ordered a drink brought for the star, and he worked with Billy as they added titles and edited the footage on a laptop computer.

Over and over the sequence played, "Hi. I'm Billy Young and I'm very sick. But I'm not here to talk about me. I'm here to talk about you. And the world. I'm just one person, but I want to remind you that everything you do matters. Please don't be cruel to other people. Be kind. Try it for just one day. And if you can do it for one day, you can do it for a week, then a month, then a year, then forever. Being kind makes a difference. I've been watching a lot of television lately, and all I ever see on the news is people killing each other. They kill each other in war, on the street, for many silly reasons. I know I can't change everything, but I wanted to ask everyone to please, just stop being cruel. Let's see if we can build a world where people are kind to each other. Let's work on it together. Thank you."

Joe barely listened to the words. Instead, he watched Billy's eyes, centers bright with excitement, edges filming over.

* * *

The commercial aired on live television and the internet the following week. Billy was at home now, receiving hospice care. He was on all the major networks, prime time. The video had even gone viral online. They watched the initial screening together, just the three of them: Joe, Teri and Billy.

A Crystal Clay toy commercial followed Billy's spot, but Teri was quick to change the channel. Joe rolled his eyes. Billy was exhausted by the excitement and fell back on his pillow.

A week later, the legion of late night shows parodied Billy on his bed. Sick young children began their speeches talking of noble virtues and ended by demanding several strippers be brought at once. Joe interpreted this as evidence they had made their impact on the culture.

"I hope I made a difference," Billy said, the muscles in his face not responding. Was he smiling or frowning? Joe couldn't tell. He had seen this effect of slow death before, years ago when his father had faded away.

"Of course you made a difference, Ace," Joe said. "If cruel people make a difference then kind people make a difference. You did great."

Billy's eyes were closed and his head was back. Joe was unsure if the boy had even heard him.

* * *

That was the last time they spoke. Billy faded in and out of consciousness but said nothing more. Joe and Teri sat by his bed, listening to him breathe, holding hands. One morning Joe left to get coffee. When he came back, she met him at the door. "It won't be long now."

She sounded both relieved and disappointed.

Joe nodded. He threw the newspaper down on the table, pointing to it and then leaving the room. He didn't want to see Teri's reaction.

"Billy's words inspire," the newspaper headline read. The front page was filled with a screen shot from Billy's commercial, framing his gaunt face and weak smile, the Crystal Clay next to his head on the pillow. Along with the story of Billy's message were letters from children around the country discussing their ideas for world peace.

"By the way," Joe called back to her, "I noticed that the stock for MajorCo toys had dipped slightly."

"Stocks go up and down all the time," Teri said.

"I know. But I liked it anyway."

"Let's go read it to him anyway. Maybe he can still hear us. MajorCo Toys losing a few cents in the market might make his day."

7

Nina scrambled to her feet, awake in a second.

Security guards from the mine were lined along one side of the village, rifles lowered. A short thin man stood in their midst. He looked out of place, a scholar among thugs. He called out in Huapi, "I need to speak to everyone."

Ndiko was walking toward the line, all guns tracing his path. Nina held her breath.

"That's far enough," the man said.

Ndiko stopped. "Where did this come from?" he asked, pointing to the soldiers.

"Where are all your villagers?" the short man said.

"You speak Huapi?" Ndiko asked.

"Obviously. Now answer my question," the man said.

"This is it," Ndiko said, noticing that the remaining Huapi and Nina, less than a dozen people, had gathered. They stood hunched, eyes watching the guns.

The short man shook his head and wiped his glasses on his shirt. "All right, then," he said, "Please listen carefully. This is your first and final warning."

Ndiko lowered his hand, palm down, calming his tribe. The scholar spoke loudly, his Huapi perfect. "We are coming here to claim this land, to use all of it for the mine. Anyone here will be removed, by force if necessary. You must leave this area immediately."

He let this sink in.

"I need to make sure you understand," he yelled. "This land is no longer yours. You must leave. Go to the mission or somewhere else in the jungle or enter the city. You cannot live here anymore."

"Who are you?" Nina asked him, speaking Spanish.

The man tilted his head, surprised to hear his native language. He responded in kind, "That's not important. We are doing you a service by issuing this warning."

He switched back to Huapi.

"If you do not leave this area immediately, you will not be safe." He paused uncomfortably. "You will be killed."

"This is our land," Ndiko said. "You are thieves! We have nothing left. Please."

The man ignored him.

"Why the warning now?" Nina asked in Spanish.

The man replied in the same language. "Situations like these are never without their absurdities."

"Away," the man said to the guards. They left, walking backwards, guns trained on the unarmed Huapi.

8

Later that night, Teri and Billy were sleeping. Joe was still awake, watching television with the sound off. Teri mumbled to herself, fitful and tense. Billy's breathing was slow, difficult. Joe watched him grinding down, wishing he could catch the boy's breaths and save each one.

Joe started to nod off, springing back up in his chair. Staying awake this long was difficult; he was still weak from his attempt at monasticism. He didn't want to fall asleep, he wanted to be with Billy to the end, though he couldn't say why.

Billy was breathing slower, his mouth open wide, totally slack. His lips were chapped and the hiss sounded raw, more like air escaping from his lungs than forced out.

The primal core of Joe's brain could sense what was happening. He had never heard the sound before and yet it was still somehow unmistakable: the sound of dying breaths, the death rattle. Another exhale, dry, empty.

The rattle sounded again, slower, softer. Joe let his tears come. Rattle, slower, softer. Teri tossed in her sleep as her only son let out his final rattle and was silent. Teri whimpered but didn't wake.

Billy moved no more. Joe turned off the television and quietly left the room.

* * *

Later that evening, Joe retreated to the hospital lobby, letting Teri say goodbye to Billy. The people from the funeral home were on their way. He turned on the television with the sound barely audible and ignored it while leafing through a magazine, staring at the pages but unable to read at all.

"And a moment of sad news tonight," the television news reader said. Over her shoulder a still frame from his commercial hung in space: Billy's gaunt face on a pillow, next to the piece of Crystal Clay. "Billy Young, the boy who stole our hearts with his innocent video message of peace and love, passed away last night. He leaves behind his mother and a generation who will find his words of hope inspiring for their entire lives. A shame."

She paused a moment. The still frame of Billy's video was replaced with a cartoon picture of a chocolate bar. "Next up, the chocolate-only diet. Some say it works, others say it's bunk. What do the experts say?"

Joe shut off the TV and walked outside, staring up at a starless sky.

9

Ndiko gathered his tribe the night after their warning. "I have the most difficult request for you."

The remaining ten villagers listened.

"I beg you all, please travel down the road and join with the god Lardesus, as the others have done."

His request was met with protests, denials, anger.

Ndiko was ready for the resistance. "As your chief, I command you to. The pales are coming and they are going to kill us all and destroy our land. The Huapi will be no more, unless you hide under the covering of Lardesus."

Angry shouts dissolved into plaintive whimpers.

Ndiko persisted. "There is no way to stop this. There is no point in asking 'Where did this come from?' Our time has ended. Our only hope is that you pretend to swear allegiance to the false god."

He turned away.

"What about her? Your pale woman?" someone called to him, referring to Nina.

She said nothing in her own defense, but simply looked to him.

Ndiko looked into her eyes, then looked away. "She will do as she pleases. I cannot command her. She is not a real Huapi."

Nina felt as though cold water had been thrown on her heart. Though her Huapi initiation had been in jest, she felt it still held meaning. Apparently, it had not.

Ndiko continued, "I've thought about how to handle the end with dignity. Should we all stay here and be killed? Or should we run? I've never come to any answer, so I can only tell you, it would do my heart good if you were to leave. If you can't do it for me, then do it for my father and the promise I made him: that our people would not be destroyed."

Glances were exchanged for several moments. Tears streamed down everyone's faces, even Ndiko's.

One by one, they rose and hugged him.

They formed a line of ten and holding hands, trudged up the road toward the mission. None of them looked back. The last remnant of the Huapi tribe had left their land. Ndiko and Nina were alone.

"I ask one promise of you," Ndiko said to her.

She nodded. "Anything."

"When they come, you will run."

Nina swallowed hard and threw her arms around his neck.

"It would mean much to me to know that you live on," he said.

She kissed him. Tears raced down his face, sobs shook him as he coughed out words. "I'm trying hard to be brave, but that word means nothing now. I've lost. Completely and utterly. Totally. Everything I have fought for is destroyed."

He buried his face into her neck and cried like a child.

Part 14

1

Ryan Jackson and his family (two sons, one daughter, his wife Vivian, and their dog) were watching TV.

"Oh, that's so sad," his daughter said. "That boy died, the one with cancer."

A brief excerpt from Billy's commercial was playing, a voice-over announcing his death.

Jackson's sons reached over to grab the remote from their sister. "Change it!" they yelled. "This is stupid. That kid's a wiener."

"Shut up!" their sister yelled, "He's nice. You two are idiots!"

"Peace on earth," one of the boys mocked. "People should be nice to each other! Waaa!"

"Mom! Dad! Make them stop!"

Dad Ryan stepped in. "You boys shut up. If your sister wants to watch this whiny wiener, let her." The boys snickered as their father rose from his chair. "As for me, that's why they invented beer." He waddled into the kitchen.

"Honey," Vivian whispered, "you just finished your second six-pack."

Ryan ignored her.

Billy's tele-memorial ended.

"Dad, can you get me a soda?" his daughter asked from the living room.

"You got legs, don't you, girl?"

"But Dad, you're up."

"But I'm only getting some beer. You want a beer?"

"Come on, Dad."

He responded by belching extremely loud. His sons laughed.

"Just wait until he's back and then you can go get your soda," Vivian told her daughter.

"Mom, I hate when he's like this. He drinks and the boys gang up on me."

"Oh, honey. It's just his way. Be patient."

The television show continued, but Ryan did not return.

Vivian tapped her daughter on the shoulder and winked.

"Hey, fat ass!" Vivian yelled. "What's taking so long?"

Suddenly, the rest of his family could hear Ryan cursing from the kitchen. He started softly but quickly the obscenities built in ferocity and volume.

"What the hell is your problem?" his wife called, still sitting.

The father's shouting continued and her children's giggling dissolved into concern. This wasn't Daddy's stubbed toe or spilled beer. Something was seriously wrong. Vivian started to push herself off the sofa when her husband stormed through the living room and down the hall toward the garage, his face flushed red.

"Oh, no!" he boomed. "Oh, no. No you don't!"

"Ryan, what is it?" Vivian called after him.

"The last damn straw! That's what it is!"

"Honey?" his wife said, finally standing. The children looked at each other, half smiling, nervous.

"Turn the TV off and go to your rooms," Vivian commanded. She followed her husband into the garage. "What are you doing? You're scaring me."

"Damn bastards threaten my family," Ryan grumbled as he tossed aside boxes.

"What are you talking about? We're all fine."

"Of course," he said, pulling his hunting shotgun from its cabinet. "And as long as I'm around, you always will be." He loaded the weapon.

"Honey. Stop. Tell me what's going on."

Ryan brushed her aside, and headed back toward the kitchen, weapon in hand. His children scattered in his wake.

"Go to your rooms!" Vivian screamed. "Ryan! Come back! Please!"

He smashed through the front door and left it open.

She ran to her eldest son's room. "Where's your brother?"

"In his room."

"Get in here, all of you. Now!"

"But mom, you said…"

"Everyone in one room! Now!"

All the children arrived.

"Mom, is Dad okay?"

"Of course he's-" She stopped herself. "I don't know," she whispered.

They could hear shouting outside. One sounded like their husband and father, possessed by a demon. The other voice they couldn't recognize.

The family listened tensely.

"Hand me the phone," Vivian said to her son. She dialed frantically.

"Hello, what's your emergency?"

"My husband."

She wanted to appear strong for her children, but her voice shook. Her children's eyes were as wide as their little faces could make them. The sight of their fear bit into her heart.

"What's wrong with him?"

Gunshots exploded outside. The children clutched together and screamed.

"Ma'am, are you okay? Ma'am?"

"He's shot someone! Or he's been shot! Get here quick!"

"We'll send a patrol car immediately. Stay hidden."

"Hurry! I'm here with my children!"

She hung up the phone and clutched her babies as they sobbed quietly. She tried to comfort them with shushes, but it had little effect. She said a silent prayer that they would all live to see the sunrise.

Footfalls crunched the gravel on their front walkway, then clomped onto the porch. Someone was entering their house. Her children clung to her, moaning, weeping. Their fingernails raked her skin. One of them had wet their pajamas.

Ryan Jackson found his family huddled on the floor in his eldest son's bedroom. They were shaking, the children's faces buried in their mother's nightgown, clutching at the thin garment and exposing one breast.

"My family," Ryan smiled. "Don't worry. I won't ever let anyone hurt you. Daddy loves you and will always protect you." He sat on his son's bed, aiming his shotgun at the door. Thin trails of smoke rose from the weapon's barrel.

Vivian looked up at him. "Ryan? Love?"

"Damn bastard," he said. "Dumping those toxic toys in our trash."

"What are you talking about?" Vivian said. "Who was? What toys?"

"Remember that boy, the one who had cancer and made that speech on TV?"

"He was just on. What does that have to do with anything?"

"How do you think he got brain cancer? The damn thing was sitting next to his head on the pillow."

"Honey," Vivian cried, "maybe he always had it. Maybe it was in his genes." Tears were running down her face.

"Or maybe that toy gave him cancer. A boy that young doesn't just die unless something is really wrong. Don't you think? I mean, those weird colors? Did they do any testing on it? And would we trust the government if they said they did?"

"Ryan," her words were stuttering now as she began to sob, "what did you do?"

"Self-defense."

She choked out the question. "Who?"

"Our neighbor. Taylor. The bastard. He was trying to dump those toys in our trash. He knew they were toxic, that's why he wanted them away from his kids."

"Mister Taylor?" one of their sons asked, crying. "He's dead?"

"That's right," Ryan said, leaning over the bed to pinch his youngest son's cheek, "the bad man is dead. Daddy killed him because I love you." The shotgun cradled in his arms leaned over, the vacant barrel staring Vivian in the face.

"Self-defense," Ryan Jackson said, sitting up straight.

Vivian sobbed as her husband stared down the hall. She squeezed her children against her.

Suddenly flashing red and blue lights splattered about the room. A white floodlight beam swept across the window.

"Drop your weapon and exit the house!" the police yelled through a bullhorn.

"Maybe we can sue," Jackson said, rising from the bed and walking into the hallway light.

"It's time for our piece of the pie. Hell, everyone does it."

He turned the corner into the living room, still mumbling as he went out to make his final stand, his family in tears behind him.

2

For Teri and Joe, the week after Billy's death passed like a slide show, lacking transition from one scene to the next.

They were sitting at Teri's kitchen table, selecting a coffin.

They day of the funeral was overcast, no rain. They stood together and held hands long after the ceremony, long after everyone else had left.

The night after the funeral, they were both drunk at Teri's home. She touched his hand and he touched hers, they both stared into each other's eyes. They giggled and cried.

"What a dumb idea," Teri said, speaking for both of them, quickly lifting her hand from his. Joe was already asleep, face down on the table.

* * *

A week after Billy's death, when the slide-show effect to the days ended, and time progressed more smoothly, Teri spoke to Joe earnestly.

"Joe, I never asked you for money. I know you would give it to me in a heartbeat, but I never asked because of my pride. Now, I'm asking. Just a small amount. Airfare. I need to get away for a while, I just need to go. Go somewhere and rebuild."

"You name it," he said. "I'll get you a round-trip anywhere in the world."

"I'm only going to need one-way," she said.

Joe's face betrayed his heart.

"I think we over-played the platonic hand," Teri said, grasping his arm gently. "I understand why you wanted to, for Billy's sake, but I needed someone, and I still do. I'm going to go find him, but I can't do it here."

Joe nodded, understanding.

3

"What the hell is all this?" the manager of the MajorCo Toys store yelled. His gold name tag vibrated in tune with his wavering voice. "These boxes are from the shipment three days ago! We're supposed to put out new merchandise in twenty-four hours. Guaranteed. Get everyone in here. Now!"

The stock supervisor called in his team. The lanky teens fidgeted nervously.

"Listen, people," the manager boomed. "We've got a job to do here and that's put out the goods. When a shipment comes in, it needs to be available to customers the next day. The very next day! Got that?"

The stock supervisor, standing behind the manger, nodded to concur.

"This isn't hard, people," the manager continued. "This isn't rocket science. Put the stuff out when it comes in. Don't make me come back here."

"Sir," one of the stock boys raised his hand.

"I can't believe we have questions about this! What?"

"Those boxes contain the Crystal Clay toys. They cause cancer." The other teens mumbled their agreement.

The manager walked right up to the boy's face and pointed his finger an inch from the teen's nose. "Son, I don't care if it's asbestos wrapped around nuclear waste. When the shipment comes in, it goes out on the shelf immediately, got that?"

The boy swallowed hard. "With all due respect, sir, you stock the shelves. I'm not touching that crap." He yanked his MajorCo Toys apron over his head, balled it up and threw it at the manager.

"Screw this job. And screw you." He walked out.

The manager folded the discarded apron. "Okay. You're fired. Who's next?"

"Me, sir." Another apron flew at the manager, covering his reddening face.

"Fine. Get out. Next?"

The remaining employees were silent.

"Good," the manager said, exhaling. "Now I don't have time to watch you all put them out, I've got other stores to take care of. But I want these handled. Now. So do it!"

The team quickly dispersed. The manager turned his contempt on the stock supervisor. "It's up to you to get them in line."

"Yes, sir. Of course."

After the manager left, his car tires squealing in the parking lot, the supervisor shared a smoke with his team on the loading bay.

"What a jerk," he said. "I'm not touching those Crystal Clay toys. He can yell all he wants."

"You might lose your job."

"So what? Better than losing my life. Friggin' Cancer Clay."

4

Ndiko and Nina slept under the stars, the two of them alone, waiting for the end. They held hands gently, trying their best to ignore the noisy racket from the mine.

"What will you do when they come to kill me?" Ndiko asked.

"You ask me that every night," she said. "I still don't know."

"Will you abandon me?"

"Just stop. No more of these questions."

The air glowed brighter as the sun rose. Ndiko drifted back to sleep. Nina was awakened by the miners screaming back and forth in Spanish. The machines were revving up to their full capacity. The noise throughout the night was bad. In the day it was worse.

She left Ndiko and sat in the middle of the village, stretching, trying to remember positions from a yoga course she had taken in college. She'd never felt more relaxed than during that class, she'd loved it, but never made the time to pursue it further. Now she improvised, but without soothing music or the calm voice of a trainer, she found it impossible to purge worry from her mind.

Voices were coming closer. She ducked down and peered in their direction. Several men were approaching. The short man who had issued the warning was with them.

"Burn the huts," he said. "Kill the natives if there are any."

The evil smell of smoke and gasoline wafted her way as they lit crude torches.

Nina slithered into the scrub, staying out of their sight. One by one, the flames swallowed the Huapi homes. She reached the far end of the village where Ndiko was sleeping.

"Ndiko! Wake up," she whispered, frantic. "They're here!"

She pulled him to his feet.

"Come on," she hissed, dragging him into the brush.

"Follow me," he said, leaping up.

He darted into the jungle, crashing through the foliage, holding his arm back as long as he could to prevent the branches from whipping against her. They ran, heat and smoke of the fire chasing them.

He stopped and turned, pulling her toward him. He stepped between her and the village. For an instant, she saw the sorrow in his eyes as he looked back on his burning home. Over his shoulder, through the growth, she watched the Huapi settlement annihilated. Calmly efficient, the group of men burned each hut, while others patrolled in lazy circles, guns ready.

When the last hut was set ablaze, the men stepped back, watched, and laughed.

Nina noticed Ndiko's heaving back. He was breathing deeply, trying to control himself, his hands wringing around his spear's shaft.

One by one, each hut crumbled into a pile of kindling. The men cheered, shook hands, and slapped each other on the back. Just as efficiently as they arrived, they left. A loud roar and crack announced the machines clearing a way to the mine.

"Come on, Ndiko," Nina whispered, "let's leave. You don't need to see this."

"It's the only home I ever had. My people's land," he said. "I refuse to look away. I've failed. I must watch."

Nina sat down, leaning against a tree. She willed herself to sleep against the noise and smells.

* * *

She woke up in the evening, her mouth dry and her belly grumbling. Ndiko was still staring from their hiding place. His home was nothing now but a flattened circle of ash.

"They've gone," he said.

She stirred. "We should get something to eat, to drink. We should hide."

Without looking away from the wreckage, he handed her a bowl of water, and some slices of fruit. She took the nourishment gladly.

"This is the end," he said. "Do you still wish to stay?"

"Yes."

"Why?"

"Why did you stare at them doing that to your village?"

"I had to. Someone had to see it."

"That's why I'll stay."

5

"Well, I'm keeping mine," the obese woman sitting on the talk-show stage yelled to the audience. They booed and screamed and jeered at her. Crystal Clay stars hung from her ears. Crystal Clay crescent moons circled her wrists on bracelets. Various other shapes hung on braids curling around her neck and down her ample bosom and ample belly, surrounding her in a gaudy rainbow aura.

"You idiot!" someone in the audience yelled. He stood, waiting for the jogging host to arrive with the microphone. "I just have one question. Don't you know those things cause cancer? Aren't you afraid of your children getting cancer like that poor boy on TV?"

The audience hooted and cheered and nodded. They stood and clapped with their arms extended in front of them. The host shrugged.

"Oh, everything causes cancer," the woman replied, dismissing the comment with a wave of her meaty hand, a homemade Crystal Clay ring on each finger. "How many of you smoke? Uh huh. See, you're endangering your child. My kids love Crystal Clay and so do I. We're not giving them away, we're not sending them back, and we're not throwing them out or anything. Ever! So there!"

She made a gesture with her hand that was fuzzed out by the TV censors. The audience booed.

"You know what I'd do?" another audience member said, her head bobbing side to side. "I'd sue. That company put you and your children and your whole family at risk. Take them for all they're worth!" The comment was received with thunderous applause.

"You know, that's a good point," the host said, pointing at the woman on-stage. "A boy that young with cancer? Where did it come from?"

The audience clapped and nodded their approval.

6

Ethan Scherr's desk was covered in legal briefs and scientific magazines. He leaned forward, head in his hands, thumbs caressing his temples as he mumbled at the speakerphone.

"It's nonsense," he said.

"You know that," the speakerphone responded. "I know that. But no one believes it. Even our retail workers are talking union because they don't want to touch the stuff. But the consumers are worse. There's an army of lawyers and they're going to sue and they're coming at us with everything they've got. They smell money and lots of it. They want it bad. Like blood in a pool of sharks."

"You think even a jury would buy this? It doesn't cause cancer."

"But the belief that it does is so widespread. It's just rumor, but it's moving like wildfire."

Scherr let out a heavy sigh. "All right. Call me back if there's any progress."

He hung up, only then noticing the figure in the doorway.

"What do you want?" Scherr growled.

Joe Vera stepped into the room and swept his arm around the office, decorated with MajorCo logos, trophies and photos of business triumph.

"To watch this crumble. To watch it fall into dust."

Scherr pushed back from his desk. "You want to watch this crumble? This that made you a millionaire? Do you know how many people long for the American Dream? A dream that you got by pure luck and now you want to spit on?"

"My dream does not have to be another's nightmare."

Scherr waved him away. "Oh, please. Life always has its losers. If it's not someone else, then it's you."

"We had no choice, did we, Ethan? If it wasn't us, someone else would have mined the land. Is that it?"

"Yeah. That's it. Now I don't have time for this. Get out."

"I think you better listen to your own advice. Crystal Clay is not coming back."

"I can prove it's safe. In a court of law."

"You think people will care? You once told me I'd be amazed what money buys. I am. But money isn't the real power. Want is. With or without money, want drives everything."

"You're such an idiot, Vera."

"No need to get hostile," Joe laughed. "I'm not the real enemy. I'm not the one who took you down."

"Took me down? Please." Scherr stabbed his finger at Joe. "I've got plenty of fight left. It's just begun."

"Good luck. Your customers want a refund. With interest. I tried to fight the raging river of desire, but it was useless. Now it's your turn. People want to sue you for your money. And their want runs deep and strong. You're up against a force of nature now."

Scherr's face shook as his cheeks burned red. He pushed a button on his phone. "Security. In my office. Immediately!"

Joe reached over the desk and grabbed Scherr's suit. "The river of want has been diverted by Hercules to clean up the mess we made! Don't you get it?"

"You're nuts," Scherr said, shoving Joe back. "Out. Now."

Joe left, his every step shadowed by two burly security guards.

7

The television:

The newsreader frowned and lowered her tone. "And tonight we have a sad story to report. Another Crystal Clay killing has occurred in our city, bringing the total nationwide death toll to sixteen. People everywhere are wondering how they can get rid of the toys, which are believed to cause cancer. Calls to MajorCo Toys Corporation have not been returned. However, the company did issue this statement: 'Crystal Clay toys are one hundred percent safe. Any information to the contrary is ludicrous rumor.' Despite assurances, people are determined to dispose of the toys in any way they can. Even at the expense of others."

The image showed the darkened outside of a suburban townhome at dusk. Singing mourners huddled over candles.

"This time it was the family's teenage son who took an assault weapon and went on a rampage through his neighbors' house.

Why? His neighbors, lifelong friends of his own family, had given the boy's brother a Crystal Clay toy for his birthday."

That somber image quickly changed to Ethan Scherr shoving his way through a crave of reporters, the newsreader providing the voice-over. "Ethan Scherr, Chief Marketing Officer of MajorCo Toys and the man responsible for Crystal Clay's mass production, has been subpoenaed in a class action lawsuit against the toy manufacturer."

Security officers pushed back reporters as they yelled to the crouching Scherr.

"Mister Scherr, is it true that Crystal Clay causes cancer? How do you feel that polls show most people referring to your product as Cancer Clay? Is it true you pushed Crystal Clay onto market, bribing officials so you could bypass safety regulations? Is it true? Is it true? Mister Scherr? Mister Scherr!"

8

At the monthly meeting of the Americas Business Conference, the new Palaguan Prime Minister, a leader of the recent revolution, pounded the table. The small plaque, "Palagua," popped into the air.

"We are not a dumping ground for the toxic waste of the United States!"

One of his older advisors whispered in his ear. "Until you realize that is our destiny, you will forever be swimming upstream. Now calm down, you fool."

The U.S. representative smiled. "I simply feel that it is logical to put them back where they came from. Hell, we'll even pay you for it."

The Prime Minister's eyes glistened with anger. "Perhaps, if you are going to return what came from our country, then I should return the bullets that came from yours."

The American's smile disintegrated as the reporter's stall high above tittered with laughter. He attempted to knock down the Palaguan with a gaze.

The conference moderator pounded his gavel and shouted.

"It is resolved. So moved by the United States delegation and upheld. The mineral sold as Crystal Clay, having been determined to have unknown and possibly cancer-causing properties, will be returned to their origination in Palagua at the expense of the United States government."

The Palaguan entourage stormed out.

9

The television:

Outside an enormous suburban home, Ethan Scherr pushed his family through the reporters, clutching a travel bag. Questions and camera flashes assaulted him from all angles.

"Mr. Scherr, did you have Crystal Clay safety-checked? How do you feel knowing you've given countless children cancer? Where are you going? What is your official position? Does MajorCo Toys have enough money to cover the return-to-Palagua program mandated by the Americas Business Conference?"

Scherr's lawyer led his family through the crowd. Scherr followed, holding Cory's hand, who held his younger brother's hand, who held his mother's hand. The train, head down, chugged forward, jostled from all sides.

"Mister Scherr! Mister Scherr!"

The footage dissolved, showing two men sitting at a desk.

"Welcome back to your source for non-stop market discussion. What you just saw was footage of Ethan Scherr, executive of MajorCo Toys, the man who introduced Crystal Clay to the world. Once the brightest star in the business community and the market's darling, now in very hot water. MajorCo Toys stock, a stellar performer over the past year, took a nose dive recently, hitting many people in the pocket. What's your advice, Dan?"

"Jim, when a plane is going down in flames, the only solution is to get out. The recent news that Crystal Clay causes cancer-"

"But there is no scientific evidence that Crystal Clay causes cancer. A few people get shot, and it suddenly becomes the truth? What is wrong with everyone? Where's their common sense? This is a conspiracy started by big-ticket trial lawyers looking to get their percentage."

"Would you let your children play with the toys? We all saw that boy, the one who did the be-kind-to-everyone video, died very quickly. He had the toy on his bed, right next to his head. And he had cancer. Remember that?"

"But that doesn't mean-"

"Okay, let's ignore the truth of the world and note the truth of the market. People think Crystal Clay causes cancer. It doesn't matter if it does or not. They think it does. That means they're going to stop buying it. That means that MajorCo Toys stock is going down fast. Sell this turkey. Sell it all and sell it fast."

Click.

Joe shut off his TV and sat back. His new apartment was a tiny place, but big enough for one.

He kissed his fingertips and touched them to a framed picture of Billy, smiling broadly, holding up his Crystal Clay necklace.

10

Ndiko and Nina lay together on the flattened plain that once was the Huapi village. Resting on their backs, they stared at the stars in the brightening sky.

"Why are they waiting?" Ndiko asked. "What is taking them so long to come and kill us? After the burning, I thought they would be here soon. It's been quiet the past few days."

"I don't know." Nina squeezed his hand. "Maybe they feel there's no hurry."

"No hurry? That doesn't seem in their nature. The pales worship speed."

Before she could reply, the ground rumbled. They both sat up. The sound of trucks approached, a roaring louder than the mine's activities ever had been before. The ground shook so violently, Nina hoped it might instead be an earthquake or volcano that would kill them. My God, she thought, did they bring a convoy of tanks?

Ndiko yelled something to her, it sounded like, "Run! Leave here!" but she couldn't make out the words over the noise. Instead, against any reasons available to her conscious mind, she followed him as he dashed toward the cave entrance to meet his enemy.

The space leading to the Huapi's gift from the gods had been widened and blackened around its edge. Tracks led into the opening. Mining equipment was strewn everywhere.

The thunder from down the road grew louder, deafening. Leaves and branches showered them as the trembling shook even the healthy ones loose.

Ndiko planted his feet in front of the cave entrance, his back to it. He leaned down and gave Nina a tender kiss on her lips. He had moved so quickly and smoothly, the gesture took her totally by surprise. He smiled at her in a way that shocked her, in a way that she felt his alpha-male persona was incapable of. A sensation of freezing rain flowed down her back, followed by a feeling like warm wine entering her blood.

He stepped away from her and raised his spear high above his head, screaming, defiant to the end.

The lead vehicle rounded the turn in the forest. It was an enormous truck, snapping the highest branches, filling the entire road from side to side, from jungle floor to canopy. The hair on the back of Nina's neck rose, the sound arousing primal fear.

Ndiko charged forward.

"No!" Nina yelled, chasing after him, into the sound, into insanity, into death.

Mid-stride, Ndiko released his spear with such force, he nearly toppled over forward. The blade shot true toward the driver of the truck, who ducked to the side. The spear-tip ripped a spider-web across the windshield, but did not penetrate. Instead, it bent and broke, tumbling down the side of the cab, to be crushed beneath its wheels.

His back to Nina, Ndiko raised his fist and cursed at the truck looming above him, its wheels carving trenches in the soft earth as it plowed forward.

She rushed up behind him, then leapt in front of him, holding her digital camera before her, the picture of Chief Maubombo on the preview screen, using it as a ridiculous attempt to ward off the trucks.

She screamed. The convoy barreled toward them.

Ndiko stepped beside her, and grabbed her free hand.

They could feel the hot breath of the truck through its grille.

Nina, you idiot, she thought to herself, why didn't you run?

The grille filled her sight now.

She closed her eyes tight, waiting for the end, praying one of the few universal wishes of humanity: that death be quick and painless.

The truck sputtered and stopped, close enough that she could feel the heat of its engine radiating onto her face. The roaring thunder had stopped. Except for the clicking of the cooling engine, the jungle was silent, still.

Every muscle in her body twitched. She slowly opened her eyes. She looked up at Ndiko, who met her surprise with his own terrified glare. His gaze quickly moved to her camera, a tiny image of Chief Maubombo in her outstretched arm all that stood between them and the massive truck.

"Magic," he whispered. "Thank you, Father."

The silence was broken by the sound of the cab door opening; the driver was exiting the vehicle.

They peeked around the front of the massive truck.

The driver leapt out of the cab, leaving the door open. He stumbled as he stepped down and collapsed into the mud. When he stood back up again, Nina saw he was wearing a light blue protective mask over his mouth and nose.

The driver noticed them and backed away, hands in the air. As he reached the rear of the truck, he turned and sprinted toward a jeep bouncing down the road. Identical, massive trucks stretched from the cave as far back as Nina could see, a frozen convoy trailing to where the road entered the jungle. The trucks were all stopped, each of their drivers leaping out. All of them wore protective masks.

The jeep gathered up each driver and kicked dirt in a rooster's plume as it sped back the way it had come, toward Palagua City.

The air was still again, quieter than Ndiko or Nina had ever remembered it. The mine was silent as a corpse.

They listened to the birds, the insects, their heartbeats.

"I can't believe I stayed," Nina said in English.

Ndiko looked at her confused, then quickly turned to the cooling trucks. He circled the lead vehicle, then climbed the side of its cargo bay. Looking down into the compartment, he screamed.

"What is it?" Nina asked.

Ndiko didn't reply, he was looking down the row of trucks, howling joyfully.

"The gift from the gods!" he yelled to her, jumping down. "It is full with the gift from the gods! Some are still in their raw shape, others molded! Each of the other machines is full, too!"

"Stand back," Nina said. She found a release lever on the cab and pulled it, dropping the storage bay hatch.

A rainbow poured out as the shards of the gods' gift cascaded from the back of the truck. Ndiko screamed and thrust his hands into the heap of color, light exploding all around him.

"They've been returned!" he screamed, the crystals piled high in his cupped hands. "They've been returned!"

He threw them in the air and laughed as they crashed down to earth.

Together, Nina and Ndiko bellowed to the sky, to the sun and into the jungle, a whoop without words, a victory scream. They cheered until they were hoarse.

Then they began the tedious work of carrying the crystal, armful by armful, basket by basket, back into the cave where it came from.

The End.